MW01100530

Chanticleer

OF WILDERNESS ROAD

A Story of Davy Crockett

The Meridel Le Sueur Wilderness Book Series

Little Brother of the Wilderness:
The Story of Johnny Appleseed
Illustrated by Suzy Sansom

Sparrow Hawk
Illustrated by Robert DesJarlait

Chanticleer of Wilderness Road:
A Story of Davy Crockett
Illustrated by Gaylord Shanilec

The River Road:
A Story of Abraham Lincoln
Illustrated by Susan Kiefer Hughes

Nancy Hanks of Wilderness Road:
A Story of Abraham Lincoln's Mother
Illustrated by Dina Redman

Chanticleer of Wilderness Road

A STORY OF DAVY CROCKETT

Meridel Le Sueur

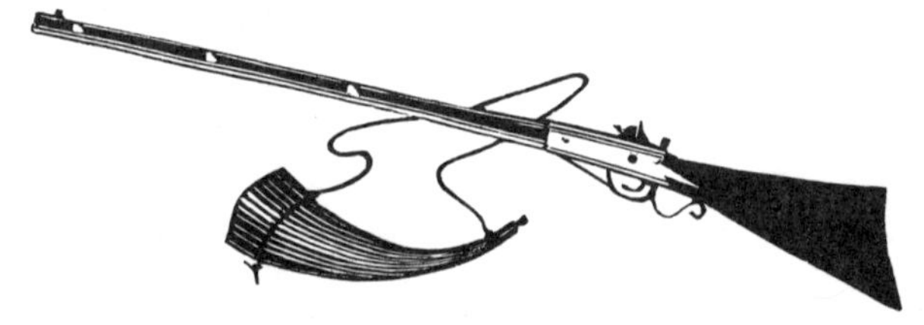

ENGRAVINGS BY GAYLORD SCHANILEC

DULUTH, MINNESOTA: HOLY COW! PRESS
1990

Photograph of Meridel Le Sueur by Judy Olausen.

ISBN 0-930100-35-2
Library of Congress Number: 88-45372

First Printing, 1990

Publisher's Address:
Holy Cow! Press
Post Office Box 3170
Mount Royal Station
Duluth, Minnesota 55803

Distributor's Address:
The Talman Company, Inc.
150 Fifth Avenue
New York, New York
10011

This project is supported, in part, by a grant from the National Endowment for the Arts in Washington, D.C., a Federal agency.

To our Irish Grandmothers and Grandfathers,

WILD GEESE, FLYING IN EVERY RISING,
OVER THE GREAT LITTLE, DEEP SHALLOW,
TALL SHORT, RIGHT AND WRONG,
MUDDY AND CLEAR RIVER OF THE PEOPLE.

Contents

THE CHANTICLEER

of the Settlement

Being the account of Davy Crockett's family. His reported death. The pesky varmint Peddler. A Basswood Ham and a Thimblerig game. Davy says, "I knowed I wasn't dead." Christmas Eve frolic. Memories of the past when Davy was a lonesome wilderness lad. Robbie's first Christmas shot. A bear hunt in the Shakes.

Walk Tall, Talk Tall

IT WAS THE TIME of the fat bears, my grandmother said, the Christmas around 1820, when in Ameriky we had just finished the Revolution and the War of 1812, and everything was go ahead and get up, Yankee Doodle Do and Yankee Doodle Done.

Tom Jefferson had made the Louisiana Purchase, after Napoleon was licked to a fare-you-well, and the country was lying big and wild with the animals in the thickets, watching the people coming over the Wilderness Road, looking through the Tennessee gap and knowing men and women had to be bigger than they ever were before.

Well, it was the Christmas, she said, when she lived near Polly Ann Whirlwind Crockett, the wife of the

Chanticleer of the Settlement, David Crockett. They had only five children then, and Davy had been gone a week, gone over the river to get a keg of powder so his next to the oldest son, Robbie, could fire his first Christmas Eve shot. They all thought he had been lost in the icy current, and Polly said, "I told him not to go; the river's a mile wide from hill to hill and we might as well starve and Robbie never shoot a gun, as for him to freeze to death or get drowned."

"If anybody'll turn up, he'll turn up," said Robbie.

And my grandmother didn't spend much time before she told you who Davy Crockett was, if you didn't know already. "He was the yaller blossom of the forest," she said, "who could talk tall, walk tall, tough as a hickory nut, strong as a bear, wily as a fox. He was one of the men with bark on, who must be men of gumption and gusto to go in and out of danger, strike a blow like a falling tree, and every lick to let in an acre of sunshine in the Big Woods. The Chanticleer of the Settlement, a ring-tailed roarer," she said.

You might take it my grandmother liked this Davy Crockett and you wouldn't be wrong.

For he was one of the hackers, hunters, swingers of the ax, the builders, tall talkers, long walkers into the sunset, a terror to kings, one of the first-rate men of Wilderness Road, half horse, half alligator, and a sprinkling of steamboat, and such as don't likely grow anywhere on the face of the universal earth, just about the backbone of America.

It was a hard life in the wilderness, my grandmother said, and rather than cry, you laughed your head off. When you were freezing in winter, you sat around the Big Fires and chewed the fat and what didn't happen you made up until, in the wilderness dark, there was a tall wind walking, and a hurricane dream ripping through man, beast, earth and forest, blowing like a bellows, fanning man to the derring-do, to dig, and hoe and build and plant and have children bigger than Davy Crockett's.

Lying for hours in wait for game, with the wildcat flashing in the darkness from the branches of a white oak, you told how you were born, making it strong, making it big, seeing yourself a Hercules lying in a giant turtle shell, rocked by water power.

My grandmother said that the story Davy Crockett told of his birth was a whangslanger and this is the way she remembered it:

"Why I sprung full-sized out of creation, talking a blue streak, and the thunder roarin' and all the varmints and the critters both leetle and large let out a moan, for they knew that breathing the limestone and brimstone of ol' Tennessee and the Nolachucky, was the greatest hunter in all creation, rocking there in a cradle made of snapping turtle shell. I had elk horns to chin myself on, a wildcat skin cover, and the cradle was rocked by water power and wind power, when my mammy lashed me to the top of the tree so that the wind would swing me about, and I was rocked high and low.

"My pappy was a sample of white oak, bark wrinkled, but flinty hard and he could grin a hail storm into sunshine. My mammy was a tall, screamin', glorious gal.

"All the Crocketts was big, from those smuggled in boats out of Ireland and listed on the ship's log as wild geese, to my grandpa at the battle of King's Mountain in the American Revolution, fightin' kings from man to son, frisky as wildcats, fresh from the backwoods, half horse and a touch of snappin' turtle. And I was BIG, and drank wild buffalo's milk, chewed corncobs, sippin' my pappy's jug and crowin' like a rooster. My shadow fell all over Tennessee. When I laughed, my mother fell over, and all the trees for miles around flattened out. I could wade the Mississip', ride a streak o' lightnin', hug a bear to death, whip my weight in wildcats. I could run faster, squat lower, dive deeper, stay under longer.

"Well, old Tom Jefferson and Tom Paine made me too big for my britches, and instead of growin' up I had to grow down to man size. My folks had to come out with an ax, and a whittling knife, and whittle me down.

"When I was six I begun to hunt varmints. We had a big dog named Whirlwind, and I got on his back and my father held up the piece while I fired off and shot a small chance o' varmints. When I was eight, if I missed my shot I went without supper.

"I grew strong and big, could run faster, jump higher, squat lower. I wooed Sally Ann Whirlwind, a streak o' lightnin', set up edgewise and buttered with quicksilver, who wore a hornet's nest for a bonnet, garnished with wolves' tails, who could shoot wild geese flying, and she beat up that wildcat of the river, Mike Fink. When there come a time when we was rammed down a hollow log; when bad times leaped on us like a catamount at full jump; disaster like a whirlwind and an earthquake, I turned on the pesky enemy, run for Congress and chased him out of all the clearings this side of Salt River, cleared out east like greased lightning chased by the crocodiles of the Mississippi."

"Well," my grandmother said, "that's the way the legend went, and nobody knows how a legend grows, everybody adding a little bit." There was the myth about his pet bull buffalo, Mississip', who could sing like a pipe organ, and his great, gaunt hounds, Whirlwind, Soundwell, Tiger, Growler, Holdfast, Grim Death, and Thunderbolt, and it was said they could bay around a mountain and tree anything with four legs.

"You could keep on all night," my grandmother said, "with what everyone told about Davy Crockett, not counting even what he told about himself."

But this Christmas the sun went down and he hadn't come back from crossing the Big Muddy for the dynamite, so Robbie could shoot the Christmas gun and so they could go bear hunting the week after Christmas. Everybody was very silent in the cabin, with all the food on the table, and nobody with the heart to eat it, and Robbie shining and shining his gun, peering down the barrel and not able to think what would happen to the whole world if anything had happened to Davy Crockett.

❧

John was the oldest son and Robbie was next to the oldest. He sat in the crowded cabin where the girls sat helping their mother, Polly Ann Whirlwind, wind a ball of flax. The babies rolled on the floor, and Whirlwind, the oldest hound, lay by the fire, his ears pricked up, his big eye rolling, asking—where is Davy Crockett?

Robbie oiled his gun for the Christmas shooting. "What are you gonna be?" they had asked Robbie since he was knee-high to a grasshopper, and he always answered, "I'm gonna be six-foot tall that's what I'm gonna be, and shoot as straight as my pappy, Davy Crockett."

My grandmother said Robbie was the spit and image of his pa, tall, and cool, and slim; he could shinny up a tree, kill a bear—a tall Irish lad of the wilderness.

He stood by his mother in the lonesome forest when only the women and the tall children were left to rock the cradle; get meat and victuals; keep warm and alive. He learned to trap meat for her, take a load on his back and pack through the woods, where sometimes you had to get down on your knees and crawl through the thick underbrush like a bear. He could go to town and trade for flour and sugar. He could mix with the frontier men there in his buckskin breeches, tough for briar and thicket. He could learn to talk tall, walk tall, and he could learn to walk small and talk little. He could walk like an Indian, soft and easy, letting the toe down and the heel follow, so he went like velvet. He could sink down in the grass and stay without moving, like his pa had taught him. He could make a sound like a turkey gobbler calling to its mate, and wait maybe three hours till he came within shot. He practiced early in the morning a call to rouse the dogs like a horn, and how to throw his voice around the ridges.

He found where the possums waited, tender as pork chops, and where the full persimmon trees were growing, and the bee combs, and the pokeberry, and the herbs for healing, so he could bring them to his ma when she needed them.

He could be still among the wild fern, watching the big turkey cock, four feet high, velvet-black satin breast and white turban, bronze and purple and gold spread of tail. He could curl up and sleep as close as a rattlesnake, and lay out straight as a gum log without winking.

When he was afeard in the wilderness, he could sing a round, or tell himself a tall story and tickle his own ribs for laughing.

"Robbie," said his mother, "stir the pot for me. Are you worried? Will he come? Will you be hunter for me if he doesn't?"

"I'll stir the pot, Mammy. I'm not worried. He will come. I will be hunter for you always."

The hounds were baying, and there was the sound of something crashing in the snow; they all ran out and, to their terror, saw Davy Crockett's horse whinnying, covered with crusted frost. "It don't mean nothin', Mammy," Robbie said, wiping down the quivering horse. "Maybe he sent it as a message that——"

"That what?" Sally Ann Whirlwind said, and nobody could answer.

They went back into the warm, bright cabin, where the gourds hung full of honey, and nuts and dried persimmons were bright in the wooden bowls, and the children peeked out from the furs, and there were piggins of chestnuts set by the fire for roasting.

Inside, Polly tried to wind the ball of flax again, and my grandmother was putting the youngest baby to bed. The silence was so big, John set up a tune;

Old Dan Tucker
Yore too late to git yore supper.

But that was too sad with the festival and frolic meal no one had the heart to touch. So John began to tell all over the tall tale about how Davy Crockett was born, and started jigging and laughing so the fear wouldn't show, and the little children wrapped in the bear fur began to laugh.

They were stopped by a knock. Davy wouldn't knock.

"Maybe it's the fiddler," Polly said, "come to fiddle a gay tune."

"Open the door you darling lumoxes, you sweet galumpusses."

Robbie opened the door and the whooz of the wind and snow brought in a gnome, bent over, and his face looked out of the snow that covered him, and one eye looked one way, and the other swept another, so he took in the whole cabin and even what was behind him as both eyes could look around corners for a deal.

"It's you," Polly said, "the Peddler."

Robbie and John began to dance around and brush him off and whirl him amongst them. "May I be totaciously exfluncificated if it ain't old Thimblerig Ouchmoucher Rattlesnake Peddler, from the North Countree."

There he was, the Yankee Peddler, real as life and twice as big, my grandmother said, who could change his face and look like something he wasn't. He could talk a mean fight, take candy from a baby, and my grandmother and all her neighbors of true grit and whole hearts, working from can't see to can't see, thought this fellow a most pestiferous, cantankerous old codger, who was against all work of any nature, and wanted only to turn an easy coonskin. Sometimes he was known as Slickerty Sam, and then again, Behemoth Grizzle, and in this story we shall see him in many disguises and with many names.

Robbie began to laugh and shout, more to forget that

Davy Crockett hadn't showed up, "Got any wooden nutmegs?"

"Got any white oak cheeses." said Polly, laughing for his wiles were well known. "Whatcha got that looks like what it ain't?"

My grandmother said he had a down look as if he was setting traps, and he could swap, sell, hornswoggle you into taking his watches, horns, gunflints, peppermints, ribbons, and dainty trash, his brag and sauce, his tinware, brooms, kettles, and pots, but he had more brass in his face than in his wares, which he said would last till they wore out.

John said, "You appear to be traveling."

"Yes, I always am when on a journey. I think I've seen you somewhere, too."

"Very likely," Robbie joked, "I've been there often! Do you have something to sell by any chance?"

"Yes a whetstone."

"I thought so. You're the sharpest blade!"

"Now cut dirt, drat you," the Peddler chased him with a broom, and Robbie cried, running, and the children screaming, "I was not born in a thicket to be scared by a cricket."

Polly chased them both, "You set now, you varmints. Let the poor Peddler set and eat."

After he had eaten, the Peddler got out his thimbles which he put on the table in a triangle, and he'd slip the pea from one thimble to the other, and you had to guess which one it was under. But the catch was that

he could roll the pea out so neat, that it was never under the thimble that you picked. "Wouldn't you like to play the little game of Thimblerig, my little laddies, just to pass the time?"

"Don't you boys gamble," my grandmother said. "He'll beat you no matter which you choose."

Robbie said, "What kind of country is there, Peddler?"

He looked at them cunningly, "Land and water mixed and single wet and dry."

"What kind of weather?"

"Oh, long spells of weather, frequently, sunshine in the day and dark at night."

"Drat you. What kind of houses in the north?"

"Oh, log slab, and the chimneys stick out the roofs."

"You won't get nothin' free out o' him," my grandmother said.

"What do people do?"

"Some work, some laze, fish, hunt, steal, and if hard pushed, buy and sell corner lots."

"Is there music?"

"Strong. Buzz of saw, sound of ax, wolf howling, cowbells, manufacturing in every household. Now, my little laddies, just one game."

Robbie said, "I got my eye on that ham for my pa, Davy Crockett. We'll play riddles, a ham against four coonskins, two out of three. What goes over the hill but doesn't eat. What goes to the creek but doesn't drink?"

"A cowbell," said the Peddler, one eye gleaming.

John said, "Four legs in the morning, two at noon, three at night?"

The Peddler scratched his chin, his head, a tear came in his other eye and he gave up.

"A baby!" they all cried, "at first it crawls, walks upright, then in old age has to have a cane." And Robbie went on, "What goes up hill and down hill, stands still all the time but goes to the mill every day?"

"I shouldn't have done this," the Peddler cried with both eyes. "It's out of my depth. Let's go back to the thimbles."

"Give up? A path!" they all cried.

The Peddler bowed low, "You win and here's the nice, juicy ham from an eastern pig, very fine."

It looked so delicious and Davy loved refined ham.

The Peddler looked cock-eyed at them all. "Did you say your pappy's name was Crockett?"

"That's the name, the Chanticleer of the Settlement," Robbie said.

"Very sad. I swear they said his name was Crockett."

"Whose? What do you know? Have you seen him?"

"Well, I'm sure I saw him stretched out and I hope he was dead because they buried him."

The cabin was still, and Robbie took the Peddler by the collar and was like to choke the air out of him, when Polly said, "We won't believe nothin' till we see. Nobody can never tell me Davy is dead. I wouldn't believe it even if I saw it with my own eyes."

But just then they heard it—a belling of the hounds,

a cry in the forest through the still, cold night. Each hound took up the cry and it belled further and further. Polly screamed and ran out in the tree-crackling, cold darkness, and all the Crocketts bayed behind her, and such a racket, my grandmother said, was a sound for panthers.

And coming through the snow-covered trees, through the Christmas night, tall, muscular and fleet, Davy Crockett swung out of the wilderness into his own cabin clearing, into the cries and the arms of his family.

"I got the dynamite," he shouted above the din. "Ain't I the yaller blossom of the forest, the flower of gum swamp? I knowed it was Christmas Eve so I jumped on Death Hug's back, whistled up a hurricane, grabbed hold of a streak o' lightnin', greased it with rattlesnake oil, and it let me down in my own clearing in nothing flat."

"Shut up, you wind bag of brag." Polly was mad now he was safe. "We heard you were dead. We heard you were buried."

"Why," cried Davy Crockett, swinging her up in his arms, "I knowed that was a whopper of a lie the minute I heerd it!"

They all looked dismayed and then they all began to laugh and the hounds laughed and the little fiddler came out of the snow laughing in his long beard and they all went into the warm cabin. Robbie punched up the fire to warm the greatest hunter in Kentucky or Tennessee, the ring-tailed roarer, Davy Crockett.

He looked at his family and gave out a big laugh so the rafter shook. "Keep me in salt to keep me from spilin'. Give me food and I'll be easy and ready for a fight, a shoot, a sail, or a turner, or a twister. Tune up there, fiddler, I'm a-roarin' to go!"

LONG MEMORY *of the Wilderness*

"WELL," SAID CROCKETT, "this is what happened. I waded through snow four inches deep, and the river looked like an ocean. At the channel I found a long log and mounted and got to an island where I kept a log to cross, but it had sunk and I had to tie my gun and bundle to a sapling and dive in the icy water for it. When I found it, I got across to the slough and had to walk with my gun held above my head to the opposite shallow shore. My feet were frozen, but my gun was dry and my bundle was dry. I changed clothes and walked the five miles to my friend's house. I brought them in two deer and insisted upon leaving the next morning cause I knew you'd be without meat. I had the keg of powder to carry now and reached the river in the all firedest cold I ever felt in my bones and marrow. I opened the way before me on the icy river trying to get where the ice would carry me but I kept falling through. I had to make two trips on my logs for my powder and gun. I made it across and I'm not dead though I was mighty nigh it, but I've got my powder and that's what I went for, and it's dry too!"

Well, my grandmother said, there were pones of corn bread, turnips, and Indian pudding with wild honey, and after the venison sizzled on sticks, and the chestnuts were popping in the fire, the fiddler set to fiddling, and all the animals set around the cabin, too, letting out a howl when a note struck them. They all danced, even the little children and some neighbors who had come in. The Yankee Peddler danced some Slickerty Sam jigs. They did the double shuffle and the double triple trouble. My grandmother did an Irish reel she hadn't done since she was four-and-twenty. The fiddler outdid himself, and Davy yelled out:

Sugar in the gourd,
Honey in the horn
I never was so happy
Since the day I was born!

When they fell laughing on the bear hides, full of food and frolic, it was time for the stories. Davy sat before the fire, the sleepy heads on his shoulders. Robbie was holding his gun till the shooting at midnight, and Davy said, "Burn my boots, if it ain't gettin' on when Robbie is gonna take his first shot at midnight, and goin' with his pappy on a big bear hunt. The thing is let go, be easy, know yore right, then go ahead. When I was a shaver I couldn't even hit a tree. I was tense as a rattlesnake."

There was a silence, my grandmother said, and Davy seemed to be wrestling with a memory, and something mighty painful to put into words for his sons and all listening. He saw himself a lone and lost boy driving eastward over the hills and far away, to Virginny, to the sea where he saw the sails flying as many masts as a western canebrake; how he almost went to London but came west with the rough, roaring waggoners, over the Blue Ridge to look through the Tennessee gap, to see the long prairie lying blue as grapes. He had learned how men used and foxed you; how you could sell your labor and not get paid; how you could be a bound boy like a slave, and go to school only one week. He had a hard time not being swallowed by the myth about him. Everyone had to swim in the great legend of the building of America. He wanted now to tell the truth about the wild geese of Ireland, and his grandfather in the American Revolution and how he had been shot by his friends, the Indians, mad at other white men who had taken their land. He wanted to tell how American democracy had come out of the forest and gained new strength as it touched the earth and the people. He started easy sparring with the myth that tracked him like a panther.

"I've talked many kinds of talk, bird and small beastie, Yankee, and southern, and Nolachucky, single, and double, and triple talk, good, bad, masked, and free, Irish and Ameriky mountain, and plain, forest, and town. Tonight I want to tell you clear how it was when I was a boy and saw that I didn't want to plant taters, hoe no cotton, pick no 'baccy or be President. I was a hunter and wanted for to roam."

My grandmother said he held them all till midnight that night, and time to shoot off the frontier salute. She said she wouldn't trust her memory for what he said so clear and plain, but that years later Polly put together all his writings—after he became a Congressman, and went to the Alamo to fight for the Republic of Texas, and died there—in a book which you can read called, *Life of Colonel Davy Crockett.*

This is the way he told it that night to his son, Robbie, and his wife, Polly, and all the neighbors of good grit and whole hearts.

"Mine was a poor but I hope honest family. I was the fifth son of a family of six sons and three daughters. My mother was named Rebecca Hawks. My grandfather fought in the Revolutionary War, in the battle of Kings Mountain and was killed in his own corn field by a tomahawk. I was named David after him.

"I was born on August 17, 1786, whether by night or

day I never heard, but I was born. Indeed it may well be inferred from my present size and appearance that I was pretty well born, at the mouth of the Limestone on the Nolachucky River. I began early to be a sort of a little man.

"My father's mill went out in a flood, lock, stock, and barrel. We moved about ten miles to Greenville, where we couldn't make it, so we moved on to Jefferson Country where he opened a tavern on the road between Abbingdon and Knoxville on the Holston near a ford, where a trail from the Blue Ridge crossed the river and wound away through the forest. All the waggoners stopped there, going both east or west, and were the greatest storytellers that ever lived. I put up their horses, served them, showed them to bed. I remained at the tavern until I was twelve, and about that time you may guess if you belong to Yankeeland, or reckon if, like me, you belong to the backwoods, when I began to make up my acquaintance with hard times and plenty of them. My father was poor and his tavern small, and he was always in debt like everybody else. So, when I was twelve, young as I was, and as little as I knew about traveling or being away from home, he hired me out to an old Dutchman to go four hundred miles on foot with a perfect stranger that I had never seen until we arrived at a place three miles from what is called Natural Bridge, and made a stop at the house of Mr. Hartley. My Dutch master was very kind to me and gave me five dollars, pleased, as he said, with my services.

"This, however, I think was a bait for me, as he persuaded me to stay with him and not return any more to my father. I had been taught so many lessons of obedience by my father that, at first, I supposed I was bound to obey this man and I stayed with him. But one day I was playing on the road with two other boys when an old waggoner, Dunn, and his two sons I had known at my father's tavern, came along in three wagons.

"I told them I wanted to go home. They said they would stay that night at a tavern seven miles from there. If I could get to them before the next morning they would take me home, and if I was pursued, they would protect me. This was a Sunday evening. I went back to the old Dutchman's house and as good fortune would have it, he and the family were out on a visit. I gathered my clothes and what little money I had and put them all together under my head. I went to bed early that night, but sleep seemed a stranger to me. For though I was a wild boy, yet I dearly loved my father and mother, and their images appeared to be so deeply fixed in my mind, that I could not sleep for thinking of them. Then, the fear that if I should attempt to go out I would be discovered and called to halt, filled me with anxiety. Between my childish love of home on the one hand, and the fears of which I have spoken on the other, I felt mighty queer.

"About three hours before day in the morning, I got up to make my start. When I got out, I found it was snowing fast. The snow was about eight feet deep and there wasn't any moonlight, and all around me snow was falling so that I had to guess at my way to the big road about half a mile from the house. I pushed ahead, got to it, and went in the direction of the wagons, but the road was under the snow too deep to leave any part of it to be known by either seeing or feeling. The snow came to my knees, and my tracks filled briskly after me, so that by daylight my Dutch master would find no trace of my going.

"About an hour before daylight, by my inner compass, I got to the waggoners, already stirring, feeding their horses, preparing for departure.

"They were very kind to me, but the wheels seemed to turn so slowly, and the country was so all-fired big, that when we got to Virginny I left my friends and set out alone on foot. Thoughts of home, poor as it was, rushed in my memory and drew me like a mustard plaster, and my anxious little heart panted to be there.

"On foot I met a gentleman returning from market who had a lead horse. He kindly offered to let me ride it to keep me from having to wade the cold water of the Roanoke River.

"Fifteen miles from home we parted and he went on to Kentuck, but the kindness of this man to a little straggling boy, has a place in my heart, and there it will remain as long as I live.

"I stayed at home the next fall when my father took it into his head I should go to school. I went four days. There was a big Salt River bully there with a gang, much older than I was. I waited for him in the bushes and pitched into him like a wildcat and scratched his face to a flitter jig. After that I left home every day, but lay out in the woods and returned with my brothers at night so my father thought I was going to school. But the master, Benjamin Kitchen, wrote a note asking where I was and the jig was up. My father was in the very devil of a hobble, in good condition to make the fur fly. I told him if he turned me over to this old Kitchen, I would be cooked up to a craklin'. He told me he would whip me an eternal sight worse. He got the two-year-old hickory and broke after me. I put out with all my might and soon we were both up to the top of our speed and I was running in the other direction from the schoolhouse. I believe that if my father and the schoolmaster could have both levied on me about that time, I should never have been called on to sit in the councils of the nation for I think they would have used me up.

"I made for the hill like a young steamboat, hid myself in the bushes, and waited for the old gentleman to pass by, puffing and blowing as though his steam was high enough to burst his boiler.

"I cut out and, at the home of a friend a few miles away, hired out with a drover named Jesse Cheek, and we set out eastward and I went on with another jolly good fellow named Adam Myers, and at Gerardstown the waggoner didn't get a back load so I set to work for a man named John, ploughing small grains for twenty-five cents a day. I thought of home and those dearest friends, nearly the only ones I had in the world—my brothers and sisters.

"But then I thought of the school house and Kitchen, my master, and the race with my father, and the Big Hickory he carried, and the storm of his wrath. It came and hung on like a turtle does the fisherman's toe, it came right slap down on every thought of home—the promised whipping.

"In the spring I got some decent clothes and decided to hang onto my journey and go ahead to Baltimore. I joined a waggoner and gave him the balance of my hard-earned money—about seven dollars. At Ellicott's mills, I was in the wagon changing my clothes, when some wheelbarrow men working on the road came along, scared the horses, and away we went down the hill. The wagon tongue broke off, snap went both singletrees, and there I was like a rat floundering about in the flour barrels, in a good way to be ground up as fine as ginger by the barrels rolling over me. But this proved to me that if a fellow is born to be hung, he will never be drowned; and further than that, if he is born for a seat in Congress he has no hope that even flour barrels will make a mash of him. All these dangers I escaped, but like office-holders, for awhile I was afraid to say my soul was my own.

"While we repaired the runaway wagon, I went down to the wharf in Baltimore and saw the big ships and their sails all flying. I had never seen such things in all nature. I stepped aboard one, and the Captain asked me if I didn't wish to take a voyage to London. I told him I would get my clothes and money and go with him. I ran back, but my waggoner told me that he would not give me my clothes nor money, and he would bind me and take me back to Tennessee. He did not let me out of his sight, walked behind me with a wagon whip. But one morning he was sleeping from a night's carousal, and I got my clothes and cut out on foot without a farthing of money.

"I was a sad boy walking alone on Wilderness Road. I met a waggoner going westwardly who kindly inquired where I was traveling and I sought a friend in him. My youthful resolution which had brooked almost everything gave way, and if the world had been given to me, I could not, at that moment, have helped crying.

"When I told him how I had been treated, he got very angry and made me go back with him. The poor waggoner confessed he had spent my money, and intended giving it back to me in Tennessee. I felt reconciled and with my new friend started west.

"We met and joined other waggoners, and went through the towns where gentlemen in tall hats and lace at their cuffs looked at us; and we sat around campfires and it was then I learned to talk big against the long space and the darkness, outgrin a raccoon, outtalk, outwalk big men, make it always juicier, outrageous, this side of lying.

"But one day I itched to see my country and my people

and said I would set out afoot, and my friend said to the other waggoners that I was a poor, straggling boy and they made up a purse of money for me, as I was a stranger on a long journey, going where it was not even a wilderness.

"I had three dollars which gave out by the time I got to Montgomery in Virginny, so I got a job with a hatter named Elijah, agreeing to bind myself to him for four years. But in eighteen months he went broke and left the country, and for this I got nothing, and was without money, clothes, or friends. I set in again working until I had a little money and cut out for home.

"I had to cross the Little River in a storm in a canoe that capsized, and when I got across, my clothes were frozen to me, but I kept going and got to our cabin and tavern late in the evening. I stood outside scared to go in. Several wagons were there for the night and considerable company about the house, so I walked big as life and twice as scared, with a waggoner, into my father's tavern. I had been gone so long and had grown so tall that they did not recognize me. I saw my mother and my sisters fixing supper and my father pouring horns of grog. I had been gone so long that they had given up any expectation of me, and they had all given me up for lost. I sat down to supper and my sisters and brothers sat at the table, strangers to me. I saw my oldest sister, Amantha, looking at me, and then she laid down her spoon, ran around the table, and seized me around the neck. 'This is my lost brother,' she said. 'This is David.'

"I often thought I had felt before, but sure I am I never had felt as I felt then. The joy of my sisters and brothers, it humbled me, and made me sorry that I hadn't submitted to a hundred whippings sooner than cause so much sorrow as they had suffered on my account.

"I was not fifteen," he wrote at the end of his life "and it will be a source of astonishment to many who reflect that I am now a member of the American Congress, the most enlightened body of men in the world, they say, that at so advanced an age, the age of fifteen, I did not know the first letter in the book.

"My father was as poor and unlucky as ever. He had a debt of thirty-six dollars and he told me if I would hire out and work out the note, he would discharge me from his service and I might go free. I did this and after working six months, I got my father's note, but I left there as it was a heap of bad company. I knew very well if I stayed there I should get a bad name. I gave my father the paper which seemed to please him mightily, for though he was poor, he was an honest man and always tried to pay off his debts. I could have gone free, but a Quaker farmer told me he held a note for forty dollars for my father, so I stayed there six months and worked this out. When I had finished, I borrowed a horse and went home for the first time. I pulled out the note and handed it to my father and the old man looked mighty sorry and said he couldn't pay it, and then I told him I had paid it off for him as my duty as a child to help him along and ease his lot, and it was a present from me. At this he shed tears, and as soon as he got over it said he was sorry he could not give me anything but he was not able, he was too poor.

"I went back to my friend the Quaker, and bound myself out and worked for clothes. In about two months something happened, I can never forget. I have heard people talk about hard loving, yet I reckon no poor devil in this world was ever cured with such hard love as mine when it came on me. The Quaker's niece came to visit, and when I saw her my heart would begin to flutter like a duck in a puddle. She was engaged so I saw my cake was dough, and I tried to cool off as fast as possible, and I began to think all my misfortunes growed out of my lack of learning.

"So I thought I would try to go to school some, so my Quaker helped me to go to school four days, and work two, for my board and schooling, so I was working and learning backwards and forwards. In no time could write my own name, read a little, and would have read more but I had it in me to go to beef shootings, sneak out for a hunt, and cut out to hunt me a wife.

"I won't tell about the widow and her ugly daughter, and how I salted the cow to catch the calf, but then I saw Sally Ann Whirlwind at a harvest frolic and I was a goner. She had a good countenance, was very pretty and could spin like a spider, and I was full bent upon her. We danced all night and I went home to the Quakers and bargained to work six months for a horse so I could go see her, for she ran in my mind day and night. The first time I went she came from a meeting with a young man and I thought maybe I was barking up the wrong tree again, but I determined to stand up to my rack, fodder or no fodder. But my girl left the other one and came with me and I saw she preferred me all hollow.

"Then I went on a hunt and got all fired lost in a storm, and I heerd somebody holler, and I ran in the blinding wind and there was my little girl, lost as I was, traveling all day, and I could have taken her up and toted her for I thought she looked sweeter than sugar, and by this time I loved her almost well enough to eat her."

Robbie said, "That was Sally Ann Whirlwind Polly Crockett, to be the mother of all of us."

Davy and Polly touched warm hands over the last baby who was asleep now. "Tell the rest," they all cried. "Go ahead." Altho they had heard it every Christmas.

"Well her ma was wrathy, and I had to take horses and my brothers and sisters and go fetch her the day of the wedding. I rode up to the door and said, 'Are you ready for me Polly?' And she said she was. I then told her to light on the horse I was leading. And she did so. But at the gate her pappy said he wished we would be married in her house, that the old woman had too much tongue, and he went back and talked to her and the old mother come out and said it was her first child to marry and go off in that way, and if we would light she would do the best she could for us. I sent for my parson and we were married and passed the time merrily, and I thought I needed nothing more in the world.

"My Irish mother-in-law gave us two likely cows and calves. I cleared a place in the wilderness, and made a cabin, and my old master, the Quaker, gave me fifteen dollars' worth of things at the store to put in it, and it was fixed pretty grand. My wife had a good wheel and knew exactly how to use it. Like all the Irish she was a good weaver, and in no time had a fine web of cloth ready to make me my first cloth britches. She was good at everything a woman could do, including children, one a year.

"We couldn't make anything on rented ground, so I quit and cut out for some new country. We had two sons already, the ones you see here, and I found I was better at increasing my family than my fortune. I thought I'd better move while I had less to carry. The Duck and Elk country was just opening up, so I packed everything on one old hoss I had, broke to halter, and we set out across the mountains, and arrived in Lincoln County, on the head of the Mulberry fork of Elk River. It was a very rich country, and it was here I began to be known as a great hunter, and to lay the foundation for all my future greatness!"

"A modest man," Polly said, laughing against his shoulder. "And then we moved on as we are always moving on with this great, this unsurpassed, this ring-tailed roarer, this mighty father and hunter. We moved to

Franklin County and settled on Beans Creek, where we are at this moment, and it is about time for our second son to shoot his Christmas gun before his father talks himself into the White House."

"Well," said Davy, "if the people want another President from Tennessee, why then I reckon I must go in for it. If they should send me to Congress I can't help it."

Polly laughed fit to kill, "A modest man! Robbie, bring out the ham!"

Robbie brought out the fine looking ham. "I won it," he said, "from the Peddler."

"Ho, Ho," cried Davy. "Who ever won anything from him?"

"Where you goin'?" my grandmother said, nabbing the Peddler by the collar as he was about to sneak out the door. She held him up like a skinned rabbit, while Davy sharpened his knives, and started to cut the ham. He sawed this way and that. "What the—why you—this ham's made of basswood, painted real cute. Why, you varmint! We may be squatters but we're particular about some things. We always expect something of a stranger, but not crocadile miracles or pesky traders in masks."

My grandmother said the Peddler looked like a fox smelling a hen roost, as Davy continued waving the knife at his sharp nose. "We moisten yore clay and make you welcome. We expect certain things. If a man spits in his face he is duty bound to say something about it. If he can't hunt, perhaps he can fight, if he can't fight perhaps he can scream, if he can't scream perhaps he can grin pretty severe, and if he can't do that, perhaps he can tell a story. But all you can do is set upon poor people on Christmas Eve and plague their spirits with a ham that isn't one."

"I only come," chattered the Peddler, "to tell you how you can get in on the ground floor now, get land and rent it out for cash money, and how you can own the whole country and live like kings."

"Some rogues are slick enough to slide on snow on the coldest night. When a tyrant takes a liberty with the natural liberty of man, it raises a Mississipp o' my blood into a perfect freshet. I'm from the upper lower fork of the great little, deep shallow, tall short, right and wrong, muddy and clear river of the People, and I'm so strong I scare myself. I sleep in my hat, sun myself in a thunderstorm, grin down the hickory nuts, swim stark up the cataract of freedom, dance a rock to pieces, ride a panther bareback, and sing a wolf to sleep and scratch his hide off, and that's what I aim to do to you. One, two, three, and out you go, and you can scream in the wilderness till all the wolves are deaf and outfox the fox."

With that they heaved him out the door and the ham after him.

"Now," said Polly, "it's midnight, time for the grand shootin'."

So they all went outdoors, Robbie with his gun polished to a fare-you-well. "Tell the bears to be on the move," laughed Crockett, as he handed Robbie the dynamite to put in his long rifle. Robbie blew through the hole to make it clear, thrust a feather through the touch hole, with a turn of wrist like Davy's, put in the bullet, filled the powder pan and then, with a long lift, he put the brassbead clearly against the farthest star, took a long short aim looking down the barrel, the star in his young sight, he pulled the great trigger. He was almost knocked down, blinded by smoke, and the hounds were hollering, and the snowy woods echoed and reechoed, as if it went off to the farthest forest, and a hoot owl cried and an animal screamed in the wilderness Christmas night.

"My son, Robbie," Polly cried, kissing him. "My new hunter, Little Robbie Crockett."

"A fine shot," Davy said, holding out his hand, man to man, to his son Robbie. "I saw a star fall. You hit the bull's eye square. Reminds me of the time—"

"Now Davy," Polly cried, laughing, "this is Robbie's night to howl."

Standing in the wilderness dark that was gleaming with snow and wildcats' eyes, they stood in their little clearing, hand in hand, and sang:

Dear little stranger,
Born in a manger,
No downy pillow under his head.
But with the poor, he
Slumbered securely,
Dear little babe in his bed.

ROBBIE'S
First Bear Hunt

THE WEEK after Christmas, Robbie, John, and Davy Crockett started out for the Shakes to find the winter bears, saying to Polly and the others, "We'll get some fat bears if we have to track them to the end of time."

"You let Robbie shoot his first bear now, and don't you hog the show, Davy Crockett!"

The hounds, Growler, Holdfast, Soundwell, Grim Death, and Thunderbolt, charged ahead ready to sniff out all the fat bears in creation. The ground was as slippery as a soaped eel.

Some people, my grandmother said, were afraid to shoot bears as you had to get them on the first shot or they might hug you to death, but bear hunting was nothing to Crockett. He said bears were as witty as men, and all you had to do was wait till they got fat, and then go after them. Then they were easily taken, for a fat bear can't run fast or long.

I don't know, but according to Crockett, the bears feed up in the falls and get into their holes in hollow trees or logs or cane houses in the hurricane, and they lie there until spring, like snakes. And he contends these varmints, with nothing to eat all winter, come out in the spring not an ounce lighter, just lying there and sucking their paws. He says he doesn't know the cause of this, and will leave it to others with more learning. "I ask no favors of a bear," says Crockett, "no further than common civility!"

They had gone about five miles, Robbie and John stalking beside Davy, and the hound, Soundwell, crying far like he could bay down anything under the sun or the moon. They sang sometimes as they walked, singing the frozen birds out of the trees. When the animals found out they were out for bear, they took it easy, for they knew that when the hounds were out for bear meat, they weren't hunting nary another thing.

They saw a bear once, too fat to run, tuck his head in his paws and give himself a push with his hind foot, and roll down-hill in the snow ahead of the dogs. He was so fat the bullet wouldn't go into him and they all had to shoot.

"That's not my bear," Davie said. "My bear I will have to shoot alone."

They hung it from a limb till they could come back for it, and already the dogs were far ahead ranging the canebrake.

They met an old New Englander who said he was afeard of bears, but he would give a powerful sight for some bear grease for his skillet and a warm hide for his bed. Davy said, "You stay here and fix a camp for our bears, and pull in the one we just shot and you'll have enough meat till kingdom come."

So the old man made a camp, building a scaffold to salt the meat, and gathering wood to smoke it. They went on into the Shakes, sometimes turning into gnarled stumps, their fur caps looking like tufted moss. They could stand without moving, sometimes they had to get down on all fours, snorting and rooting through the underbrush like wild hogs.

The lead dog was baying now, raising the yell that all the rest answered. Robbie was ahead breaking to them. None of the dogs would enter the bear's hole till Davy came up, for they knew their master so well that he could have made them seize the old serpent himself with all his horns and cloven feet. Robbie was wrathy to get his bear. The dogs were at the bottom of a large black oak and the bear had climbed the tree, for Robbie saw the tracks were going up but none were coming down. When they go up they don't slip a bit, but if they have come down, you will see long scratches from their nails.

"There's a bear in that tree," Robbie said.

Davy left it up to Robbie, who found a small tree that,

if chopped down, would fall against the bear tree, and Robbie could limber up and look into the bear hole when the small tree lodged against the other.

They chopped with their tomahawks when they heard the dogs barking at some distance. Davy said, "This bear's your'n, Robbie. Come on, John, we'll get the other'n."

Robbie chopped away alone, but the tree fell the wrong way and it was nothing but a shell anyway, so he started to chop another. But he was startled to hear his father say, "Look up, Robbie!"

Looking up, he saw the bear come out and start down the tree after him. He was the biggest, blackest, swiftest moving bear Robbie had ever been at the other end of, but he had kept his loaded gun at hand like a true hunter, and he caught it up and fired, and the bear came hurtling down like night. Deathgrip and Bearhug made a surround, rolling and tumbling, dogs and bear went to the foot of the hill, where the bear lay on his back with the dogs nipping at him, but keeping away from the teeth and the hug. Robbie reloaded and ran up, put his gun plumb against the bear, fired and killed him. "I knowed he was a screamer," he said, "but I'd rather not have got him this way."

John was disgusted, "You should get him on the first shot."

Davy looked admiringly at the huge beast. "Yore first bear, Robbie, and nothing to sneeze at." They took out their knives and fleeced off the fat. John went back with the three bears they had now, and Robbie and Davy went on. The dogs now with the wiry edge taken off them were in better humor and grit than ever.

Robbie felt like a man, having got his first bear, and walked proudly beside Davy, the spit and image, only green and wiry as a sapling. They could hear Soundwell's deep tones in the distance as the afternoon deepened.

They were well into the hurricane country now, and had to go slow because of the big cracks made by earthquakes. Tiger opened. Rattler following. The others joined in. Robbie cried, "He's up! He's up!" And they both went running. They came upon the dogs facing the infuriated bear that had turned on them. Davy was in shooting distance, but they were both shaking with the cold and the running, and Davy fired but only broke the bear's shoulder. He made a vicious lunge, tore the face of Growler, and ran into the cane. "I got to follow him Robbie," Davy said. "You could go back now. You might break yore gun here."

"I'm goin' on." Robbie said.

"You know yore right?"

"I'm right, I'm stickin' with you, Pappy."

"Then come ahead," Davy said, tearing after the hounds, and Robbie after him. For three miles they ran, trying not to fall into the big cracks, wading waist deep over half frozen creeks. It began to get dark before they caught up with the dogs who were baying, which meant they had the bear up a tree. Sure enough, they had him in the darkness up a forked poplar. It got dark swiftly, and Davy told Robbie to make a light fire so he could get an aim, but the ground was cracked all round and there wasn't much brush. Davy shot by guess at the dark spot, but the bear didn't come down, only climbed out on a limb, and that helped them to see him better.

Robbie loaded and fired and missed. Davy loaded and fired, thinking it was mighty nice to have a son shooting while you loaded. Robbie climbed the tree and with his knife forced the bear to drop to the ground, where he fell into one of the big earthquake cracks. You could just tell the biting end of him by the hollering of the dogs. Robbie came down and crept up to where Davy was rassling with the bear. Robbie put his gun against the bear and fired, but only got him in the leg so he jumped away from Davy and out of the crack, straight at Robbie, and the dogs came between, crying and nipping, and the bear fell back into the crack.

It was dark now so they couldn't see each other. "Robbie?" Davy said, afraid to shoot in the dark. "Pappy," Robbie said, "I'm over to the right." "Lie down with yore gun pointed. I got a pole and I'm gonna punch him up a leetle." Robbie pointed his gun and Davy got along in the crack aside of the bear and felt along for his shoulder, keeping away from his teeth. He made a lunge with his long knife and struck the bear through the heart, and he just sank down, and the dogs began to howl, pretty satisfied that they alone had finished him off.

They sat in the dark near the warm bear, panting, and

just found out how cold they were. Their clothes were frozen on them. Robbie was shaking like the ague. They couldn't get a fire going. Their flints were wet. To keep warm, they butchered the bear.

"We'll freeze," Davy said, "Before the night is over. We got to do the best we can to save our lives so nobody'll be to blame if we die."

"We'll holler," said Robbie, so they hollered.

"We'll jump up and down," said Davy, so they jumped up and down.

"Do this," said Robbie, and he found a straight, tall gum tree, slick and straight as a rattlesnake springing up, and Robbie took hold and shinnied up thirty feet, then locked his arms around it and slid to the bottom again, and this could make the inside of your legs and arms feel mighty warm and good. "You do it now, Pappy."

And Robbie made them do it all the night. They lost count but they must have done it a hundred times and they found themselves getting warm.

Morning came and they grinned at each other, and Davy said, "I shore got me a son!"

They skinned the bear, hung him away from the coyotes, and arm in arm went back to the camp which was high with snow and hung with the venison, and bear, and pheasants John had shot.

They had seventeen bears all together, and gave the old New Englander a thousand weight of fine, fat bear to last him all winter—rugs for the floor, covers for the bed, and grease for the griddle.

Davy was very happy. "I couldn't stand it without the hunt. And nobody knows what a hunt is till he hunts with two brave sons of his own flesh."

He had to turn away and swear at a hound so they wouldn't see that he had something in his eye mighty like a tear.

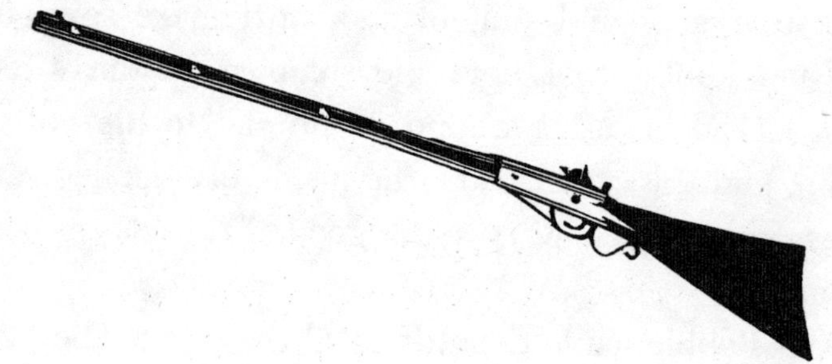

The People Speak

In which Davy meets the Peddler and a Hurricane. Moves to Shoal Creek. Goes on a strange alligator hunt. Meets Andy Jackson and fights the Indians. Runs for Congress Loses his shirt and wins with Jackson.

DAVY MEETS THE PEDDLER *and a Hurricane*

THERE WAS a tavern down Elk River, below Crockett's cabin, where hunters, traders, roustabouts, river men, gathered before harvest for long talk, and tall tales, and common doings, and uncommon gabbing. One day in high corn time, Davy and Robbie sat in the tavern trying to trade their coonskins for most anything. There were some Yankee hunters there that day, and they had all heard of Davy Crockett and were raring to hear some tall tales. The Peddler was fooling with his thimbles, slipping the pea from one to the other, faster than the eye can wink. When they all called for another horn of ale, he cutely asked, "When does the moon get a horn?"

Crockett said, "Whenever she gets a quarter."

"I never see a quarter," said the Peddler, with uncommon sadness. "All I see is coonskins, but furs is money or they used to be."

"We're all sheddin' crocadile tears for you, Sam Slick," said Davy. "You nimble-footed thief of the world. I'll grin you down someday. Got any wooden nutmegs, any calico axes?"

"I got some basswood hams," Slick said, with a sly smile.

A hunter from the north said, "I hear you can grin most any varmint out of countenance."

"Well," said Davy, "I see the politicians grinnin' themselves right into the White House. If you can grin the vote in, you can grin a possum down from a gum tree. But once, one moony and clear night, I saw a rascally old racoon on the topmost crotch of an oak, and I thought I'd grin him down. I grinned and grinned, and he sat there looking more like a racoon every minute with his stripes and rings, a ring-tailed roarer sure enough. I got into a pretty savage humor when he didn't fall, so at last I clomb the oak and, take my eyes for green grog bottles, it was nothin' but a knothole without any bark on it, a barked tree with two big knotholes in it for eyes."

Another hunter said, "That ain't nothin' to Crockett. The way I heerd it, you had a bead on a racoon and he lifted one paw and sez, 'Is yore name Crockett? Then you needn't take no further trouble, for I'll come down without a word.' And the critter walked right down from the tree, considerin' hisself shot!"

There was thunderous laughter and slapping of thighs. "That ain't all," says Davy. "I reached down to pat his head and told him I was complimented and wouldn't hurt a hair o' his hide. And he said, 'Seein' as how you say that, I'll jist walk off for the present, not doubtin' yore word, d'ye see, but lest you should kinder happen to change yore mind!' "

"Ha Ho Ho Ha!" they all roared, and now Crockett was smoking and raring to go. "That ain't nothin' for Crockett. Once I tamed a buffalo to come to meetin' every Sunday and roar the base of Old Hundred, and he loaned the choir leader his horn for a tunin' fork. I tamed a she-wolf so she would do my yawnin' and shakin' for me. But one morning I had walked eight miles and had such an appetite I could have ground up a hickory stump, roots and all, and my peeper caught two eyes lookin' out of a cave, and I darted over skulls thick as pumpkins, and there was an old strappin' he-panther settin' on the end of his tail and grinnin' at the bare bones as if he was twice as hungry as me. He licked his teeth and growled, and I grated thunder with mine, but he gave me to understand that he was the terror and big eater o' the forest, and that his teeth were o' the crosscut saw disposition, and his stomach a forty-stone mill, and that he would make a ghost of me instanter. We both advanced grittin' and growlin'. We slammed right together and I give him an upward blow, a gouger in the bread basket, turned him on his back, tied his tail in a knot, made him repeat the Bill o' Rights and the Constitution, taught him all sorts of civilization, and took him home. On a dark night he'll light me to bed with the fire of his lookers; he brushes the hearth with his tail; does all the heavy work; rakes the garden; does all my extra screamin', curry-combs the horses; and lets my wife hackle flax upon his teeth. If he don't then feed me for dinner to a flock o' hungry wildcats in winter!"

Then the Peddler had to tell about the freezing North. "Why it is so cold we wuz buried in the snow and slept under forty-two blankets; got lost and nearly starved to death; the hot biscuits froze before you ate 'em; our words froze and were thrown behind the stove and the next spring our ears burned when they thawed out. Even the shadows froze to the ground and had to be pried loose with pickaxes."

"Why that ain't so very cold," Davy said. "Sounds to me like a great cry and a little wool. You don't look to me like such a much. Tell a better one or I'll make you run so fast your shadow will run to find you and you'll see your back in front and be in danger of running over yourself."

"Well, I got lost on the prairies once, in a blizzard, and I knowed I'd freeze, so I slit the belly of my horse and got in and pulled the ribs around me, and went to sleep warm as toast. I woke in the morning to see the sun red out of the carcass, and a couple of coyotes snigglin' round, and I waited till they were close, thrust my arms out the ribs, grabbed them both by the tail. They took to flight and away we went, sliding in the carcass over the

frozen hills, and at my front door I let go the tails, and my wife chopped me out, gave me coffee, and I milked the cows."

"That's a whopper," Davy said. "What else can a Yankee do?"

"A Yankee is a self-relying, prime, braggin', strivin', swappin', wrestlin', quizzical, astronomical, poetical, and criminal sort o' character. I'm a live Yankee, sirs, sharp as a briar, wits polished keener than a needle."

"What can Yankees DO," Robbie asked.

"Yankees get up and do, Yankee doodle do—Yankee doodle done. Can do almost anything and everything. He sets up that style of shop. He's an animal made of hard knocks, and of the stick out and up and dressed up school. He can preach, keep store, shoe horses, teach school, doctor, love the girls, build sawmills, singing schools, make steamboats, and patent medicine, and churches, plow the earth, mount the air, make laws, cheat and lie a granite rock out of countenance. Go to Congress, write books, recite the Bible from Genesee to December. A great inventor . . . Well he is. Trade with him and see, and the above isn't a priming to what he can do."

"With his hand in your pocket," Davy said. "I traded with him once and got a basswood ham. You're a slick one. Grease your head and pin down your ears, and I could swallow you at one bite."

"You'd have mighty fericacious pains in yore innards if'n you did," the Peddler said, his mouth shut tight as a miser's, and one eye looking one way to see his advantage, and the other like a weasel looking round a corner.

It looked like there might be a fight, so someone said, "Let's snuff a candle." They all went outdoors, set a candle in the crotch of the tree. The Peddler took aim for a mighty long time, fired and missed. "Leave it to Crockett," the hunters said. "No slang whanging," Crockett said, took aim, snuffed the candle, leaving the flame burning brightly.

Suudenly there was a distant, terrible thunder. They saw that a thick haze had crept along the trees and the wind from the fires of the soap kettles was laying back like a wildcat's ears. Before they could move, a big wind struck, and the trees of the forest shot through the air like feathers.

"Hurricane!" they shouted, leaning in the wind. Crockett and Robbie had already taken off, running toward the cabin.

They were behind the hurricane, so when they arrived the sun was shining, the roof was gone, the cabin leaned crazily, the chimney was riven through, and Polly Sally Ann Whirlwind was walking up and down her roofless cabin, the newest baby on her hip, and the little boys playing on the floor.

"These things come in pairs," Davy said. "Maybe there'll be an earthquake." So they all slept outdoors that night, curled up close together as rattlesnakes. The next morning Polly knew that look in Davy's eyes. "I don't believe we'll stay here anyway. We've been here most two years. Over south, over the mountains, there's thick soil and deep hunting."

"Oh!" Polly cried, "I heard of a woman there found a panther right in her cabin. She seized the panther by the throat and wrestled him into the fire and the panther, choked and blinded, ran up the chimney, out on the roof and fled."

"So you see," Davy says, "it goes to show the panthers are better behaved there."

"And the wildcats," said Robbie, "have the look of rattlesnakes on their faces, and their eyes shine like fires."

"Well," said Davy, putting his arm around his two tall sons, Robbie and John, "now we've got three big hunters. When the animals hear us comin' they'll run for Texas!"

My grandmother said that Crockett and Robbie went ahead, built a cabin, sold their place for fifty dollars and one morning, in the fall, when the persimmons were ripe, my grandmother took over some dried meat and corn cakes, and Polly wept a little on her shoulder because they were going so far in the wilderness, where never a granny woman would be coming to help in the winter sickness, or help the new babies to come, or lay away those that did not live.

"Buck up," my grandmother said. "Our breed were called the wild geese, the gray geese, because they fly high, they are strong, and always fly against the wind. If the value of skins keeps going down, and the taxes up, I'll be following you in the spring. We've come this far, over the sea from Ireland, where we got used to hunger and hangin'. We come over the Smokies, through the great gap, into the swamps and the Shakes. It makes my sap rise how we get pushed and pushed!"

"That's the naked, skinned, green truth," Davy said. "Yes, sir, we got to turn and do another kind of runnin'. Yes, sir." He poked Robbie and yelled to the hounds waiting to be off, "We'll have to run for something."

"For land?" said Robbie.

"For Congress."

"Huzza," my grandmother shouted. "Huzza for Crockett for Congress."

"Maybe," said Davy, "I'll have to be President. Mighty ripe time for us bushwackers, trappers, squatters, Wolverines, Pukes, Buckeyes, and all to send us a coonskin President to the White House. Too much velvet, lace and beaver hats."

"It's bad enough," Polly said, "you runnin' west without runnin' east too."

"Robbie here, can go west, and I'll go east, and between us we'll hold the country for the people."

My grandmother waved her apron, "For the Frolics and the Fightin' the people have Crockett."

"Look at that old gal there, some grandmother," Davy said. "You get the people to vote for Crockett. Why, children, she used to have such a cough that it used to set the cider barrels rolling about the cellar. Did I ever tell you about the Indian? Well she used to go to chaw hickory limbs, and one mornin' while she was settin' on a stump, an Indian walked most audaciously up to her, collared her by the cap, and started preparing his execution iron in true valor to carve off Granny's top knot. Now Granny, being a reg'lar fotched-up Kentuck gal, didn't mind her scalp no more'n a cherry stone; but her family cap war of the true Martha Washington pattern and she'd sooner parted with life, cough and all. So she hung out her eyes at him obstinaciously wicked, while he squinted at her scalpaciously cruel. He grabbed her, and were just going to scalp her, when she give one of her all shakin' coughs that sent him rollin' in the leaves as if he were struck by an earthquake.

"The old gal set extendin' her eye at him and chawin' hickory considerable. He thought this were a cough producer, so he begun to chaw, and Granny grinned and gummed at him. But the Indian were still determined to have a drink of her vital revolutionary sap, so he crawled toward her. Then Granny's revolution begun to rise in her at the rate of old '76, and she give a cough at him that would have silenced a forty-eight-pound cannon, and she gave him full galloping consumption."

"Now, Davy Crockett, you ought to be ashamed," my grandmother cried, but nothing could stop Crockett.

"She's a Granny, an all-screamin' glorious gal, can jump a seven rail fence backwards, dance a hole through a double oak floor, spin more wool than one of your steam mills, and smoke up a ton of Kentucky weed. She can crack walnuts for her great-grandchildren with her front teeth, and laugh a horse blind. She can cut down a gum tree ten feet round, and steer it across Salt

River with her apron for a sail and her left leg for a rudder!"

"Get out o' here," my grandmother shooed him with her apron, and so, all laughing, the hounds belling ahead, their plunder packed on one horse, they were off into the forest. Polly carried the baby on her back; Davy went ahead with the one-year-old on his shoulder, and Robbie carried the two-year-old sitting on his shoulders. The girls, carrying guns, brought up the rear, and they all sang to keep from crying:

Over the river to feed my sheep
And over the river to Charley.
Over the river to feed my sheep
On buckwheat cakes and barley.

It took three days' walking, singing and story-telling to get to their new home. Robbie said the animals peeked out of their holes and said to each other, "Thar goes Davy Crockett—Scram! We never miss Davy Crockett and he sure as fire never misses us!"

When Davy saw the fear in Polly's eyes, or any of his children afraid of the night dark as they rolled up and slept, he told some tall tales. When the hounds slept in the far circle of darkness, and America stretched unknown, without road, or bell or book, it was time to tell a few.

"Now you may think we go traipsin' around, but I mean to tell you that there's no human flesh in all creation more partial to home and the family circle, square, kitchen, barn, log, hut, pigpen or fireplace. Every morning of lightin' my pipe I like to be given all colts, wildcats, children, and wimmin an all squeezin' hug all round. Did I ever tell you about my daughters now?"

The girls all screamed with pleasure. They loved to hear his great legends of them when they felt most small and lost.

"Well, I always had the praise o' raisin' the tallest and fattest gals in all Ameriky. They can outrun, outjump, outfight and outscream any critter in creation. The oldest one growed so etarnal tall that her head got nearly out of sight when she got into an all thunderin' fight with a thunder storm that stunted her growth; and now I'm afraid that she'll never reach her natural size. Still it takes a whole winter's weavin' to make her walkin' and bed clothes; and when she goes to bed, she's so tarnal long, and sleeps so sound that we can only waken her by degrees and that's by chopping firewood on her shins."

Forgotten was the darkness and the unknown cabin in the woods toward which they walked as the children hugged each other. "That's Sapinna Wing, a long drink o' water."

"Well," went on Davy, burping the newest daughter, Judy, the flower of Gum Swamp, "my other daughter has a body like flint rock, her soul's lightnin', her fist a thunderbolt, her teeth can outcut any steam mill. At six she has the biggest foot and widest mouth, and when she grins she is so splendiferous, she shows most beautiful internals, and can scare a flock o' wolves to total terrifications. My other daughter, Katy Goodgrit, is a fighter. A bear sprung at her for a bite o' Crockett meat, very tasty to bears, and she grinned a double streak o' blue lightnin' into his mouth and it cooked the critter to death as quick as think. She brought him home for dinner. She'll be a thunderin' fine gal when she gets her natural growth if her stock o' Crockett lighnin' don't bust her biler and blow her up."

Just then there was the screamin' of a panther in the deep forest and all the children felt their flesh creep, and Davy went on in a loud voice, and Robbie punched up the fire.

"I had a sister I never told you about, she was of the Doing Good, Go-to-Meetin' Womananity. She could preach a few, too, her pulpit a rock, and her sacrament the pure natural element of Adam. Her words could make the coldest heart open like a clam, and a bad man's hair stand straight up and bow to her! When she sung a psalm all the trees were pipe organs and a hurricane the bellows. She was always on hand with heart, arms and pocket open, and has been the traveler's sun, star and salvation for the last years.

"The biggest heap o' good she ever done was when she walked the frozen bank of Columby River for fifteen days, livin' on nothin' but pure hope, to hunt up fifteen men lost in Colonel Fremont's caravan that was scattered by a snow storm. And that gal never rested head nor foot till she explored the hull country, rocks, ravines, holler logs, stickin' as true to the chase as an alligator, till she found 'em, and piloted 'em safe to Californy. She wore out seven constitutions, three consumptions, and four fevers, keeping travelers from freezing, famine, wolves and vultures."

Something was creeping towards them and Robbie got up with his gun and the hounds stood with bristling pelts but the firelight frightened whatever animal it was and Robbie said, "Tell about your marryin'. Tell that."

"Oh," Polly said, "that old story."

But you could see she was pleased, nursing the youngest baby, and Davy looked at that strong, enduring woman over the firelight, and he said with love, "That woman who is your mother, is a streak o' lightnin' set up edgewise and buttered with quicksilver. She chased a crocadile till his hide came off. I met her in the forest after she killed a monstracious big bear, and helped her carry it from head to tail. She still wears that varmint's hide for a shift. When I married her I made her a bearskin petticoat, an alligator's hide for an overcoat, an eagle's nest for a hat, with a wildcat's tail for a feather. I rung off a snapping turtle's neck for a hair comb, and we outscreamed a catamount and sucked forty rattlesnakes' eggs on our wedding night. The minute I laid eyes on her I knew I meant to try my steel against her flint."

"And I knew he was a whole steamboat," Polly said,

looking at that tall roamer in the wilderness, over the bright, protective fire.

"Three miles from her house I began to scream, and could see my voice going through the air like flashes of lightning on a thunderbolt."

Polly was in the story now, "And it sounded most beautiful to me for it went through the woods like a hurricane. I ran out and climbed a tree and waved my bear-skin petticoat splendiferously, and when that tall hunter, Crockett, come runnin' through the woods and caught me, he give me such a hug my tongue stuck out a half a foot."

Davy took the story up, "She turned white as an egg shell and I see that her heart was busting as I ran up like a squirrel to his hole and give her a buss that sounded louder than a musket. She was like a tame pigeon. Her Sunday bonnet was a hornet's nest, garnished with wolves' tails and eagle feathers, and she could drink out of a branch without a cup, shoot a wild goose flying, wade the Mississippi without getting wet."

"I told him," Polly said, "that I could not play the piano or sing like a nightingale but I could outscream a catamount, and jump over my shadow. I had strong horse sense and could weave a pair of pants that would go on the Smokies, knew a woodchuck from a skunk."

"And I said, 'I'm Davy Crockett and I am yours without any fustification.' I married her, took her into the wilderness, and made a little clearing in the midst of the wood and I thought we'd be alone but a tribe o' children came flocking in and now one—two three—I can't count 'em."

"Ten," they all shouted.

"And we're alone no more," Polly said.

And the next morning they all started out, walking and singing and telling tall tales through the pathless wilderness.

CROCKETT MEETS UP WITH *Old Hickory*

AT THE HEAD of Shoal Creek, where the Crocketts now lived, there were many bad characters, and no law. There were hideouts for river bandits, thieves, counterfeiters, and horse stealers, gangs who lived in the caves, and bad white men who captured fleeing Negro slaves and resold them into captivity. The settlers had to set up a kind of government of their own, my grandmother said, and Davy Crockett was elected magistrate. He used to just speak out the warrant for the arrest of a bad man, but Tennessee became a state about then, and Davy became a Squire, so it wasn't fitting to just yell, "Catch that man and bring him to trial," for now the warrants must be in real writing and signed by Squire Crockett, the records kept in a book. This was bad business for Crockett, since up to then, he could scarcely sign his name.

So now he began to learn to spell and read, working at night, and he said, "I got along relying on natural sense and my judgments stuck like wax as I gave my decisions on the principles of common justice and honesty between man and man, for I never read a page in a law book in my life."

There had to be a heap of law giving, my grandmother said, as the Scotch often didn't like the English who had put down Scotland, the Irish didn't like the Scotch who had helped keep Ireland down. Nobody liked the Quakers, and the Germans did not like anyone; some liked towns; some wilderness; some thought themselves better in lace, velvet, and beaver hats, with brick houses and slaves. Some were proud of their strength in the wilderness, their rude dirt-floored cabins, split log churches, windows greased with bear oil, linsey woolsey and tanned buckskin, and a hankering for freedom, every man under his tree at sundown.

My grandmother often told me there was a new kind of man walking the woods. There was Old Hickory Andy Jackson, who beat the British at New Orleans, and Davy Crockett, who beat the Dutch anywhere, and they were both to leave their brag in the bark, figuring out, day and night how a man can grow taller and a woman stronger and sweeter, how to let in the sun to fall equally on all, in the tall forests and the long prairies.

There was the hardwood, limestone, blue grass country, prairie and woodland, beavers, otters, looked like enough to feed a lodge of Humanity, but the price of pelts went down; there was no salt; some people didn't want others who were poor to vote; every seven years there was a depression; and all a poor man was sure of was children and taxes.

The People began, my grandmother said, to dream a tall dream of sending their own buckskin hunters and squatters to the White House, and it was a dream they were to make come true.

It would be too happy to think that among all the new neighbors, who were all true grit and whole hearts, there wouldn't be the Peddler turning up again, in another face, this time named Joe Jenkings Hardpuss Snatch. He had a down look as if he were setting traps, and he was much better eating than he was at taking game. He had a vociferous eye when it was open, but he never looked a man in the face except in the pitch dark.

He went on a hunt, didn't shoot a bear, but took his part so they were all glad when he sent word he was going to have a big alligator hunt with tame ones in his pond, and the neighbors should all come and bring a saddle and bridle.

So when the day came, Davy and Robbie started out for Mr. Snatch's cabin with a dozen Suckers, Wolverines and strangers. They found his door fastened, no smoke, so they pounded at the door and poked their Kildevils through the cracks to poke him out but he didn't come out. So they put their butt ends upon a log and waited for him until the sun went down and they began to smell a rat. Crockett put his foot against the door as if he was kicking a mammoth, and it jumped off the hinges like a reformed office holder. The pesky squatter had gone off with all his plunder and had chalked out half a dozen great alligators on the wall. They saw they had been fooled and then they biled right over. Crockett jumped up and hit his head on the roof. "Let's sally out and go after him, and if I get a sight of a piece of him as big as a mosquito's liver, I'll plaster it with cold lead." They all set out, some ran to Gum Swamp and some clean to Salt River, but the pesky Peddler was gone. Crockett went home in an uneasy temper, and swore terrifcasciously in his sleep, so Polly had to put a hot brown bread poultice on his stomach to keep his gall from busting. The next morning he chalked the Peddler's name over the door, and vowed that he'd lick him in t'other world if he never found him in this!

Crockett was against stealing the Indian lands, but when the Creeks attacked Fort Mimms and Andy Jackson was leading the soldiers, Davy had to argue with

Polly about going. She begged him not to go. She was a stranger in their new home, and the little children would be left at a lonesome and unhappy time if he went away. "It was mighty hard to go against such arguments," Davy said, "but if a man waited for his wife to tell him to go to war there would be no fighting." Polly seeing he was bent on it, cried a little, and turned about to her work.

The harvest was in, and Polly was used to being alone in the hunting season so he volunteered for sixty days and went into the Creek nation as a scout, a skilled woodsman who knew the ways of the Indian as well as his own.

Wanting to find out the right of it, he slipped through the lines, silent as an owl, and went to the camp of the Creeks, straight to the Creek Chiefs, and asked them direct, "Why do you fight us?"

The Big Chiefs answered, "The white man sold us things that were not real, and made it out that you could buy and sell land which we know is an untruth as land belongs to the Great Spirit and is for the use of Man. The white man's tongue was hung in the middle and wagged both ways."

Davy said, "Did this man wear a high collar and a beaver hat?"

"Once he looked like that, and with windy words got us to sign a treaty, and we are not used to papers."

"Did he have a pack on his back and one eye going one way and one eye the other?"

"And his tongue going both ways. He sold us a wooden ham."

Davy yelled right out, "Slickerty Sam Thimblerig Snathum Grizzle, that tetociously scoundratios, pesky varmint. I'll see Old Hickory Andrew Jackson about this."

Just then there was an awful scream like a panther, and Davy knew it was the Creeks' leader, Red Sticks, and jumped on his horse, rode all the next day to get to Jackson.

In camp the whole army had gathered outside the Creek nation waiting, hungry, the winter cold as Christmas. All day and all night there was Old Hickory striding up and down on the bluff, a wound in his shoulder, sick, with a hungry army. It was right here that Crockett began to tell taller, stronger, quirkier stories for the hungry men listening to the sounds of owls, the Indians in the darkness. It was a time when man has to honey himself together, store up spirit like beeswax for winter fat.

Crockett poured out his memory like a bottle of brandy, poured it into the hungry gullets and the fearsome eyes. He brought out all his childhood and instead of not going to sea with the old captain, he pretended he went, made up an old sailor, named Ben Hardin. You never could believe that you could remember so much or make up so much that you can't remember. And Old Hickory walked up and down on the bluff, talking against the hunger and the lonesomeness and the sadness of Squatters having to fight Indians, wondering what for. You tell everything that has happened and everything that hasn't happened. You wheedle and tickle the spirits of man and make him see it all very, very small, or very, very big. As you can see trails that nobody sees, you make them see history that you don't know will come true even. You imitate old waggoners long dead, the old German and Quaker, the hunting and fishing, and you make it easy; the cold and ice of the river holds you like a mother and you sit talking to the fishes, flat on the bottom, comic as anything, plucking off the fish as they go by. You tie up the beasts that lurk in the darkness, by the tails, and hang them up to smoke. You travel with talking animals. You do anything until that hunger look leaves in the darkness and everyone is rocking and laughing and punching each other and saying, "It's nothing to Crockett. Know that man Crockett? A fool for luck and a poor man for children! Can you beat it?"

The fearful animals began to talk; they heard that the crickets were saying Crockett, and the Indians tricking them, appearing and disappearing, became tall tales and legends.

Andy Jackson was walking back and forth. One morning when the men were hungry and the food didn't come, Davy Crockett could see the red top knot shining like a blaze of light on the hill and the men said, "Go tell him," so Davy moved toward the blaze of light, and it wasn't the sun on that wintry day, it was a red-headed man just like him, in a fringed buckskin shirt, moccasins, and coonskin cap. He had a face like a gnarled branch, and eyes like knotholes, and lightning for veins, and vinegar and pepper salted him down in anger; an old oak aimin' to live like a free man and shooting lightning at all the Snickering Sams.

Davy Crockett and Andy Jackson faced each other both straight weathered like old hickory, burned and kiln baked, with heated ideas of freedom in both.

"I'm Davy Crockett."

"I'm Andy Jackson."

"I come to see you about the shape of the country. I don't wear a collar around my neck and follow no man."

"I'm collarless, too, Davy Crockett. You're a man of great grit."

"You're a slangwhanger yourself. You're the yaller blossom o' the forest, and when you stand up to fight, every soldier jumps ten feet in the air, cracks his heels, and crows like a rooster, and neighs like a stallion."

"I heard, Davy, that you can hold a buffalo out to drink, look a panther to death, stand three strokes of lightning without dodging, and put a ball through the moon."

"Slightly exaggerated," Davy said. "But now I'm a heap taller because I am the delegate from the men down there."

"The settlers and hunters," Andy said, "are the hickory strength of this army. You have the great grit and gumption."

"It's a pleasure to hear you praise us for we aim to go home now, our sixty days being up, and nothing to eat,

our clothes in tatters, and our wives thinking us dead and gone."

Andy Jackson began to smoke, "You're the finest volunteers I ever saw, volunteer to fight and then volunteer to go home. Over my dead body you will."

"Hold your horses, General. We aim to get a chance o' honey, change clothes and hosses, and come back to the fightin'."

"I'm head of this whole pock-marked, runnin', fightin', fuddlin', army and nobody is goin' home!" Andy yelled, smoking like a tar pot.

"We're hungry and we're goin' home for a spell." The men below the bluff saw the light from their eyes flash and lock, and the steam spouting from their boilers. "We aim to come back. We haven't eaten for days, and like the

Irish get used to hangin', we got used to it, but we got to put up some more fowl and bears for our children."

"You're a stubborn man, Davy Crockett. I'm a stubborn man. We should stick together."

"We should stick together, Andy Jackson, like burrs. I don't know no more of politics than a goose does of ribbed stockings, but you and me could shake the bank and be a caution to Silk Stockings."

"I aim to run for President," said Andy Jackson.

"Well I might aim at it myself if I don't starve to death in the Creek war."

"Well you better not aim to take your men home or you'll be shot. I'll put my soldiers on the bridge and shoot you down as you pass over."

"I wouldn't do that, Old Hickory. I wouldn't do that."

The next day, the drafted men were behind a cannon mounted on the bridge. They were strung up on both sides. They had their flints picked, and their guns primed, and started over. They heard the guards cocking their guns and they cocked theirs. They marched boldly on but nobody fired and one Yankee yelled out, "Bring our knapsacks and we'll come along." Cracking jokes, they passed over the bridge, marching boldly on, and not a life was lost.

"Tho' I was only a rough sort of backwoodsman," Davy wrote in his book, "my wife and children seemed mighty glad to see me, howsoever little the quality folks might suppose it. For I do reckon we love as hard in the backwoods as any people in the whole creation."

The men got warm clothes, a bit of fat, a chance of honey of affection, fresh horses, and came back to the war, and fought to the bitter end. Davy Crockett sat beside Andy when they made the treaty with the Creeks, the Cherokees, Choctaws, and Seminoles, and was against sending them far west to the prairies, dooming huntsmen to land where they could not hunt. They surrendered half their hunting grounds and later that was taken from them, and like the Squatters, they began their long march west in what was to be called the "Trail of Tears."

Crockett felt blue leaving the Treaty tent and went down to the creek for water. An Indian was stooping to drink, and Davy didn't feel so all-fired proud speaking to an Indian. But as he watched him drink he saw the mask slip and show the shallow chops of the Peddler, one eye looking for rain and the other squinted at the chickens like a weasel's. That infarnal Peddler had been sitting right there at the Treaty in the disguise of an Indian, getting them to sign away their lands forever. Crockett let out a howl and took after him. The Peddler ran and hid himself among the Indian women and was lost to view.

Crockett was glad to be through with the whole matter and thought war was no fun, nothing but dog eat dog.

Polly had a new child to show him. "All I want," he said, "is to live in the Shakes, come home with the fire burning and Polly Ann Whirlwind waiting with another child. Hunt and stay as long as I live and love."

Robbie said, "The people are speakin' o' you for Congress."

Davy was cleaning Old Betsy for a bear hunt. "The people make a clown o' you. The Cambric ruffles pull me down, telling jokes, making me a comic. It makes me sad all over."

Robbie said, "That's not the people. That's old Cambric Ruffle whose runnin' for Congress and nobody agin him."

Davy squinted through the barrel of Old Betsy. "If they only knew I'm dead earnest behind the jokes, like behind Old Betsy, I'm aimin' straight at them. You have to put things a tall, joky way that will make people, who otherwise would hang you to the sour apple tree, think yore jokin'."

Robbie was after him. "It would be right for you to run."

"I am a great lover of my country and my people, Robbie, but not of its officeholders, grabbers, pork barrel plutocrats, psalm-singin' bigots. What kin you do, only the dead have free speech."

"If you had the floor o' Congress," Robbie said, "the people would have a voice, a tongue, a power."

"It's the truth," Polly said, "and everyone wants you to run. Our gentleman from the Cane. You'd be right to represent the people."

"You're right," all the children shouted, and jumped in the air, cracked their heels, crowed like roosters, and shouted, "Then go ahead!"

If you listened close you could hear Crockett tell his hounds, "i'd rather hunt any day than go to Congress!"

HUZZA
for Congressman Crockett!

MY GRANDMOTHER said the People called Andy Jackson and Davy Crockett to lead them out of captivity and bondage and they came. That year, the new frontier states gave everyone except the slaves, black and indentured, the vote, even if they had no property. So there was the surge for Jackson, but Crockett hadn't changed his mind about running for Congress until one day he and Robbie went to town to trade their furs for sugar and flour and calico, if they could afford it. But they got next to nothing for their skins, and sugar and flour had gone up. Cotton had gone down so a man got nothing for his year's work of planting either. Nothing seemed sure but death and taxes.

It was a bad time for this gentleman, Bartholemew Skipaway Grizzle, who was running for Congress, to come into the tavern dressed in a fawn-colored coat, with white lace at the throat and cuffs, and his well-curled wig showing beneath a hat made out of little dead beavers. It was less the time for him to make a remark about the foul odors of steaming buckskin, and of the squatters who squatted inside. Davy Crockett rose like doom in the talk and smoke and held his nose, "What is that bad smell wrapped up in a cambric ruffle that just came in? Smells to me like the smell of slaves' and other men's sweat."

Gentleman Grizzle drew himself up to five feet, and said, "I am running for Congress in this district. I own the land, the title, the cotton and the slaves. Out of my way, squatter."

Davy grabbed him by a ruffle, "Let me introduce myself. I am Davy Crockett, first-rate-and-a-half and a little past common. I can blow a wind of liberty through a pumpkin vine, and play the *Gray Goose* on a corn-stalk fiddle with any man. I kill more bear, whip more panthers. I'm a real ring-tailed roarer from the thunder and lightning country. I can run faster, jump higher, squat lower, dive deeper, stay longer under, and I aim to run for Congress against you!"

"Whoops," everyone shouted, almost blowing over Mr.

Grizzle, who forgot his manners and began to sputter like a gutted candle, "You infernal, hypocritical, scaley-hided, whiskey-wasting, squash-headed, no-souled, hay-hooking, corn-cribbing, roaming scab of the wilderness. I don't exactly recall your name, but I'm pretty sure I've seen you somewhere."

Davy from the shoulders of his voters cried, "You fodder-fudgin', vote-buyin', cent-shavin' whittler o' nothin', you've seen me somewhere for I've been there frequently, and since you can't forget what you've never known you don't know nothin'. I'm the Chanticleer of the Wilderness."

So they all cried and crowed, "Cock-a-doodle-do and dandy," until Mr. Grizzle's eyes looked like a pair of preserved beans.

"Now," said Davy, as they all found stools, "I'll tell you how to run for Congress; promise all that is asked and more if you can think of anything. Call a meeting at your house and when nobody comes elect yourself, pass some resolutions, any kind, and have them published. Kiss all the babies, wipe their noses, pat them on the head. Offer to build a bridge, a church, divide the country, create new offices, make a turnpike, anything they like. Promises cost nothing. Get up on all occasions, make a long-winded speech, composed of nothing, promising that all roads will run downhill. Talk about your country, the times that tried men's souls, rail against taxes, while you're planning to make heavier ones. Some people may consider you a bladder of wind or an empty barrel.

Once you're elected, why a fig for the dirty children, the promises, the bridges, the churches, the taxes. Some may think it pretty funny to have a hunter from the cane running for office, but it can't be any funnier than the high hats who are sitting in the Kitchen Cabinet. Let 'em have their fun. I'll push ahead and go through with it. I'll stand up to the rack, fodder or no fodder."

"Huzza for Congressman Crockett," they all cried, and took him on their shoulders and paraded through the streets—hunters, squatters, farmers, with their first candidate from the new state of Tennessee in a coonskin cap, singing mightily;

Up with your banner Freedom
Thy champions cling to thee.

My grandmother said Davy Crockett was the finest figure ever ran for anything—more than six feet tall, broad in the ax swing, with high color, a fine Irish face and long, black, hunter's hair. When he mounted the stump he made a plain sensible speech, and he traveled all over speaking plain, in cabins, at suppers, grove gatherings, taverns, churches and town halls. Giving the People that serious laughter when he said, "I've just crept out of the cane to see what discoveries I could make among the white folks. I don't mind being called a bushwhacker, they pull themselves up stream as best they can and sometimes they get there. It's a step above my knowledge, I know nothing about Congress, but I aim to see that people like us receive a just due."

He put them at home showing that, like them, he too was short of words. "The thought of making a speech makes my knees feel mighty weak. You could as well go to a pigsty for wool as to look to me for a speech. But I might just try it. My heart's fluttering as bad as my first love scrape. I have to be wary as a fox not to get my tail caught in the committal trap. Here they want to move a town and I must come out for it, but how a town is to be moved I don't know, so I go on the same plan that I now find is noncommittal."

His other opponent, beside Mr. Grizzle, was the Salt River bully, Skippoweth Branch, who slept in his hat, chewed his vittles with his fore teeth, screamed through his nose as he went to a meeting on two horses, never turning out for man or beast, sworn to lick everything he saw and walk ten miles day or night for a swindle. Full of shady doings like selling Negro slaves, robbing steamboats going down river, like a tree that grows half its roots underground and can turn up unexpected snakes in the root. His cry was, "I'll have you to know I am a hoss never rode, from the stables of Snapping Creek, shod with steel traps and rubbed down with essence of thunder cloud. I was born in the world for a special purpose, and if you put your hand on my throat you can feel grit all up and down my windpipe!"

Davy Crockett began to think he was born for luck, but it would be hard to guess what kind, and he began to take a rise when he found out the People listened to him, to tell them something about the government and an eternal sight of other things he never knew before.

Finally, at the height of the campaign, there was to be a speechin', a tip-top frolic, and a squirrel hunt with a big barbecue. Each candidate was to see how many squirrels he could get. Mr. Grizzle sent out his slaves to hunt for him. The Salt River bully had his gang. Single-handed Davy Crockett and his hounds came in with the most squirrels, but Davy was worrying about the speaking, when he would have to shuffle and cut with his opponents who could speak prime. He figured he would be polite and speak last and let the others wear out the people first and then he would breeze in with his luck.

The first speaker was the Salt River bully, and he was relying more on the cargo of codfish and free rum he had set up for everyone including the babies. He said a few words and then invited everyone to eat and drink, pointing at Davy and having everyone laughing as if popularity was worth just a drink of rum and no more.

Crockett had one coonskin and he walked over with it, threw it down, and then ordered a horn of rum, and the bullies all hollered, "Hurrah for Crockett," and the rum keeper of the Salt River Roarer forgot to pick up the skin, so Crockett picked it up and put it down again and ordered another, and then another, with the same skin, winning over the bullies with their own rum.

At the resting, some were dancing on the green and Mr. Grizzle was to be the next speaker, and he beckoned Davy to take a walk with him, and he said to Davy, "I hear you haven't much money for your campaign."

"I have the People," Davy said, "and like love it's better than money."

"Well, that doesn't butter any parsnips, now," said Mr. Grizzle. "How much would it be worth to you to withdraw from this election. I could set you up, you know, on a little land, with a few slaves, and your wife would have nothing to do the rest of her life."

"My wife would have nothing to do with me, you mean. I will get on on the products of the country, sir. Among the best products of a poor man are industrious children and the best of coon dogs; and when you gentlemen knock down the worth of furs and cotton, I can go wolfing, and shoot the wolf at the door, skin him and sell his scalp for three honest dollars and this way get along till I whip the livin' daylights out of you."

Mr. Grizzle was bothered like a fly in a tar pot and got up to make his speech, smoking like a steamboat going up-stream in a wind. He made a long, windy speech that put the people to sleep, but just then a flock of guinea hens wandered near the platform, chattering and chattering, and annoying Mr. Grizzle, who asked three times for the People to shoo them away. Crockett piped up and said, "Mr. Grizzle, you're the first man I ever saw that understood the language of the fowls. You never mentioned me in your speech, but my good friends the guinea fowl shouted cr-cr-cr-cro-kkkkktttt and the bullfrogs, if you notice, are sounding off CrO-cro-crocketttttt . . ." Everyone roared, and his goose was cooked, so he turned against Davy and began to make fun of his speeches, knowing his ignorance as well as he did himself, he said, "Perhaps Mr. Crockett will speak to you on the judiciary."

Davy said later, "If I knowed what that was may I be shot, I never heard of such a thing in all Nature." But the people roared most respectful, and Crockett went ahead, looking down on the people listening, eyes, mouths, ears, all open to catch every word. He began, saying he was like the fellow beating on the head of an empty barrel near the roadside and when asked what he was doing that for, said that there was some cider in the barrel a few days before and he was trying to see if there was any now. And he said there had been a little bit of a speech in him a little while ago but he believed he couldn't get it out now. The people all roared with a thousand mouths. He said he reckoned they knew why he had come, for he had come for their votes and if they didn't watch mighty close, he'd get them too. He told them what they knew—how they couldn't get land, buy flour, send their kids to school. He said nobody could buy him, and that unlike other candidates, if he lost he would leave them with as much as he found them; that for electioneering he had had made a hunting shirt with two pockets, one to hold a quid of tobaccy, and the other a bottle of rum, so that when the voter threw out his baccy to take a dram and listen to his speech, he could give him a chaw back and leave him no worse off than when he found him.

The people roared five minutes at this and then he

said that he came with no money and would go with none, that he thought it better to keep a good conscience with an empty purse than to get a bad opinion of himself, with a full one. And the crowd began to rock and roar and he shouted, "Liberty, she's a nice old girl and I took her in my arms and said, you're for me."

And the people shouted, "You're for us." And they carried him on their shoulders singing mightily.

My grandmother said it was a tall time, when a family by the name of Crocketaigne could flee from a French king, flee from an English king, fly against the wind across the ocean, set themselves up in the wilderness and run for Congress.

But when Davy Crockett got back from campaigning he was dead broke, his crops had been spoiled by a wind, the price of skins was so low he couldn't buy even gun powder. So his boys and some of the other settlers built a raft, cut thirty thousand staves, loaded them and started for New Orleans. But when they got to the Big Muddy, they found that none of them had ever navigated southward where the river got wide and swift and treacherous with alligators, and they were all-fired scared.

That night they got into what is called the Devil's Elbow and couldn't get out of the current, whirling round and round, and down and down, watching the people running on shore with lights, still they could not land. Davy was below in the cabin when the top fell through on him and they were floating sideways, and he could hear the hands running above, pulling with all their might until they went broadside full tilt against an island where the current would suck the boat down. The boat was turning under and water was pouring in on Davy, and he couldn't get out on the raft, which was steeper now than a housetop. He ran back to a small hole and got half way out when he stuck, it was too small and he began to holler and his neighbors seized his arms and began to pull. He told them the water was coming behind and to pull him through neck or nothing, come out or sink. They jerked him through and he was literally skinned like a rabbit, not a stitch on, but pleased to get out even without shirt or hide.

Now with the load ruined and lost, all the work of the past and the future lost, they sat happily floating down the Broad Muddy, and Davy later wrote, "I felt happier than I had ever felt in my life, for I had just made a marvelous escape. I forgot everything else but that. I felt prime no matter what happened." The steamboat picked them up amid the debris of logs and flat boats—the long work of a summer.

Polly was glad to have him back, for it had been rumored again that he was dead. Robbie said, "We heard you went straight down and when you came up you had traveled the whole river bottom and had a message from a catfish, and you weren't even wet."

And Davy, to cover Polly's tears, said, "Who said I couldn't run faster, dive deeper, stay under longer and come up drier than any man in all creation?"

So they couldn't pay the taxes, and had to move again. This time deep into a strange land called The Shakes, where a big earthquake had made it an upside-down country like some of Crockett's stories. Trees were twisted up by their roots. There were deep cracks, some islands had sunk, others risen. A river ran back upstream instead of down. Big lakes had come and you could row around and look into the nests of birds. Nothing could shake off the land and it was deep and rich. The buried woods were full of animals and snapping turtles with great heads and armored scales.

Sometimes at night the earthquake came, and they were rocked as in a cradle. Robbie said his cap was shaken off while he was planting corn. That's what he said. Indians, Davy knew, had been driven west, and he met them in the canebrakes that were so thick, sometimes you had to crawl on your hands and knees.

They started a sawmill on the river, and a flour mill, and thought they could turn a penny. But what happened just goes to show that Crockett was a poor man for luck and a fool for children. For that spring, before they sawed any trees or ground any flour, a big freshet came and washed away the mills and they had to lash the babies down on logs to keep them from floating away.

When the water went down, Davy was pretty low, but Polly slapped him on the back, and said, "Pay up, Davy. Sell everything to pay your debts. You can't let the People down. Pay everything and we will move on. We'll scuffle for more."

Davy caught her like a bear and hugged her. "Thats just the kind of talk I want to hear. A man's wife can make him pretty uneasy if she begins to scold and fret and perplex him when he has a full wagon load on his mind. We'll take a brand fire new start. Stand up to the rack, fodder or no fodder; stand up to the lick log, salt or no salt. Anyway, this part of the land is getting too much filled up."

"Go ahead," Polly said.

Just then Robbie drove into the muddy clearing with news. "You've won. You've won by one hundred and forty-seven votes. You're a Congressman!"

"Huzza for Crockett!" shouted all the big and little Crocketts.

COME ROUND

with Yankee Thunder

Wherein the People get the best of the Peddler. Wherein Davy and Robbie join the People from the Lodge of Humanity in electing the first Wilderness President. And two tall men walk tall and talk tall by a little lamp in the White House. The story of Crockett's fight for Squatter's rights. The Beaver Hats try to bribe him. He breaks with Jackson over the Indian lands. He is defeated for Congress and decides to go to Texas. To have one more hunt with Robbie and John. Fare you well, traveler, fare you well.

THE PEOPLE SEE ANDY
in the White House

AND THAT YEAR, the people of true grit and whole hearts went wild, for they had elected Andy Old Hickory Jackson as President of the United States, and Davy Chanticleer of the Settlement Crockett, to Congress.

My grandmother said it was no accident that Davy was born the year before the adoption of the Constitution establishing the new American Democracy for the natural man and his natural rights—Life, Liberty, and the pursuit of Happiness. And some people in Kaintuck still say it was Davy and the People who rose up and tacked on the Bill of Rights!

They knew there was no mistake about Davy Crockett and Andy Jackson, and the Wildpuss Nation went wild.

Around Tennessee Forest, my grandmother said, you could hear the alligators in the swamp snapping for Crockett, and the crickets Crocketting, and the guinea hens went wild—crkkkt crkkkt—and the people had a jamboree, a frolic, an old time hoe down, to see Davy and Robbie, who was going with him, off to the White House.

And it was a sight for sore eyes, my grandmother said, to see them got up like the white shirt and silk stocking gentry, and obliged to cut their gouging nails off.

The girls in their brightest dresses, the fiddlers, and hunters whooped it up in the Great Grove, dancing circles around Robbie who moved in his tight linsey woolsey like a ripe persimmon in its skin.

The speeching was fociferously tremendous, and Crockett looked mighty splendiferously strong, like a man who could beat his weight in wildcats, my grandmother said, and they cheered him to the echo when he said, "You know, there's no mistake in Davy Crockett. I'm full when my people fill me. I'm strong when you're touchin' me. I'm half horse and half alligator and a little touch of snapping turtle and mostly I'm you. I can hold a buffalo out to drink, put a rifle bullet through the moon, fight fistifferously, kick hossiferously, or bite catifferously, and I can fight anyone in beaver hats and silk stockings who wants to take our land away from us by seizure or eight percent interest. I can wade the Mississippi, leap the Ohio, ride a greased streak o' lightning to the White House, hug old Andy too close for comfort, and eat any man opposed to Jackson."

They were all fit to be tied when a gentleman in a carriage pulled by two black horses shouted out, "Hurrah for Adams!" and Davy said, "You'd much better Hurrah for hell, and praise your own country and Jackson. Who are you?"

And the man got down with the help of his slave and he said, "I can outdance you rabble any day."

And Davy said, "Tune up," and they all started to dance around the gentleman, taking hands with his Negro slave, who began to cut a double shuffle with them, and the fiddlers nigh bust a gut fiddlin':

Met Mr. Catfish
Comin' down the stream
Says Mr. Catfish what does you mean?
Caught Mr. Catfish by the snout
And turned Mr. Catfish inside out.

Sally Ann Whirlwind Polly Crockett swung him till his teeth rattled and as the others passed him down the line, they yelled:

Honor yore partner and the lady on the left
All join hands and circle to the left
The wee wee whistles and the jaybird sing
Meet yore partner with the elbow swing.

The fiddlers jumped to *Old Zip Coon, Money Musk* and *Pop Goes the Weasel.* They fiddled loud, fiddled soft, and fiddled hard, thick and fast and swift, and the girls kicked up a breeze, the skirts awhirling and the laughter hot, as they stamped sideways, bowing, knocking knees, big hands around slender waists:

All hands up and circle to the left,
Half around and back again
Coffee grows on white oak trees
The river flows with brandy O!
Choose your two to dance with you
And swing like 'lasses candy O!

When the fiddlers got to *Smoky Mountain, Arkansas Traveler* and *Weevily Wheat,* the gentleman began to get pale and grunt, and stagger and roll his knees, and they tossed him between them from shadow to light, from square to round dances, from double to triple shuffle. They danced him down, danced him under, danced him green, danced all around and over him, laughing and clapping until he crept into his carriage and had to drive himself off.

And Robbie thought he saw his face slip off a little and there was the cock eye of the Peddler, but he couldn't be sure.

The stage was ready to carry them off. Polly stood by my grandmother, brave as Christmas. "Remember a Tennessee holler is the best storm," she cried out. "Grab yourself a piece of lightning, grease it with rattlesnake oil, you and Robbie get astride and off you go."

The horses were proud as if they had voted, and the people all shouted, "Hurrah for Davy! Hurrah for Old Hickory!" and Davy shouted, "Hurrah for the people! They're fresh from the backwoods, half horse, half alligator and I'll whop any man that says different, grease his head, and pin his ears down, and eat any man opposed to Jackson."

A flick of the whip and away they went, over the hills and far away to the White House in Washington.

Davy laughed to see how green scared Robbie was, and he shouted in his ear as they jiggled in the coach like the peas in the Peddler's thimbles. "Never mind, Robbie, my old bucko, I saw two Colonels running away from the battle once. It's what you call a forced march!"

And they went over the great hills to see the inauguration of Old Hickory Andy Jackson who was going to shake the banks of the country like a hornet's nest.

Over the earth where Davy, as a boy, had walked in his moccasined feet, they went by stage and boat and locomotive. The roads were jammed, the boats were jammed, everything was jam-packed, for the People were going to see their first rock-bottom president sit in the chair at the White House.

From the Lodge of Humanity in the West they came.

From the bloody ground of Kentucky they came.

From the factories at Lowell, Massachusetts, and from the slums of New York, the people came, the Old, New, Little, Great, Small, Deep, Shallow, Big, Muddy River —the People.

This was the first time they'd won since the Revolution and the Bill of Rights, and the way it looked, as Robbie and Davy looked out of the windows of all the vehicles taking them to Washington, the whole wild west was acoming on the barn dance of progress, the western course of empire turned round, from the whole Lodge of Humanity coming to Jackson's Husking Frolic around the Washington Crib.

It seemed like the elk, the stag, and the bear were pausing to rest in the golden thickets, shouting "Huzza for Jackson!" and "Huzza for Crockett!" Robbie never in his born days saw so many people rejoicing in their strength as they did after the Revolution. Every man, woman, child, a screamer, a singer, a poet, making every morning a Fourth of July and, like a giant mother, full of pride, pouring in a great rising sap and flood to see the nursling of the Wilderness, the people's hero, Old Hickory Andy Jackson.

The night before the Inauguration in February, Mr. Adams, the licked President, a gentleman from an old eastern family, spent a painful night worrying about the floor of the White House for he saw a big-booted muddy rabble all chewing their cuds and spitting upon anything in sight.

There were bets and jokes among the broadcloth and the cocked hat about how Andy Jackson would enter the city. That night there were even hopeful rumors at the clubs of the gentlemen that he had been killed, and they trembled in their well-shined boots as if a monster was coming out of the wilderness, and they said the country would go straight to blazes, and grass would grow in the streets with a backwoodsman as President.

Davy and his son, Robbie, went with the crowd that mulled the muddy streets of February, their hope strong; as mechanics, canal builders, wheelbarrow pushers, jenny spinners, snatched at the rumors of what Andy would do when he came, laid their bets, gawked at the sights and sang, "*Push Along, Keep Moving*," when they got together, or:

> "*Come All You Bold Kentuckians,*
> *I'd have you all to know,*
> *That for to fight the enemy,*
> *We're going for to go.*"

All of which made the gentlemen of the wig and small clothes run into the buildings and peek out! Davy and Robbie sat in the smoke-filled taverns, waiting for Jackson, where everyone drank applejack and passed the news along, spit tobacco as far as a frog can jump, and smoked seegars. It seemed that they were shouting like people just rescued from some dreadful danger. They talked of aristocratic "NEEBOBS," and how Jackson would shake Biddle's Bank, and how the government would now deal justly with everyone—broadcloth and linsey-woolsey, beaver hat and coonskin cap.

They milled along and stopped to see Mr. Jefferson's books sold at auction to pay his debts. And when there was no other entertainment, they shouted and laughed at Congress waiting, too, lolling and laughing, rattling papers, everybody eating and talking.

The people recognized Davy and Robbie and shouted outside the State Building, "Make way for Colonel Crockett."

They passed through the People, smiling, "Colonel Crockett can make way for himself."

A gentleman with a little stomach, wanted to poke fun at the coon caps, kept his tall hat on and said, "I presume when you walked to Washington you met a great many wild animals on the way and I presume you killed them all!"

"Why, Mister, I come here, my son here and I, riding my greased lightnin', Bear Hug, accompanied, sir, by my private buffalo, Mississipp'. They're over now attending Congress listening to more wind than a Tennessee tornado."

The crowd roared. Davy saw he had 'em tied up and he couldn't help but make a big wind for them. "I started out with a few hurricane speeches tied up in an alligator hide and on the way I put down my bundle to hunt a bear. I found him, and killed him, and was roasting some steak for my dinner, when I heard a great snorting and scatting amongst the leaves and there was a panther making off with my bundle of patriotism. I knew 'twould never do to lose it. How should I get along in Washington when others got off all their windy talk?

"My bundle was pretty light, and the panther went off with it, and I after him at a great rate like a shooting star, and after a wrestle, I got it back again. Then I sat down and I read the Constitution to the panther, and the Bill of Rights, and tied his tail in a knot, and made him up Jackson eight times. I got to Washington with my bundle and let loose my speeches. That was the time of the big wind."

"Davy, what'll Old Hickory do when he comes?" somebody shouted.

"Old Hickory'll bring a breeze with him when he comes, and a chance of luck for the people; and he'll say Children of sorrow, from the forest, from the whip and the lash, plant your homes in the forest, for the country watches over you; your children grow around you as hostages, and the wilderness at your bidding surrenders its beasts and its flowers, its strength and its grandeur.' "

"Huzza for Crockett! Congressman Crockett!" they cried, throwing up their hats. Andy Jackson, riding down the street, coming from the wilderness alone, after the death of his wife, Rachel, thought the Huzzas were for him. Davy and Robbie saw that there he was, his red top now white as snow, tall, gaunt, wrinkled like a frosty persimmon, and his hand aching from shaking the hands of the people from the cabin and the canebrake, from plantation and farm, slave and free. Tears filled their eyes as they saw him tall and thin, sitting his horse so excellently, his hand light, his carriage easy. That old ring-tailed roarer from the West, the old, scarred, thin, hell-for-leather Old Hickory, and the people never forgot him riding in alone, their own son. Later, the carriage was drawn to the Inaugural by six white horses, with soldiers and music, and Old Andy was disguised in a long coat and beaver hat, but his hawk nose and sharp eyes looked out upon the sea of people. The old soldiers made the Indian war hoot owl cry, and some neighed like horses, and some flapped their wings and crowed like roosters, and they hugged each other—the prairie men and river men and mountain men, the timber women, and swamp women and village and plantation women. The sun broke through the clouds as the carriage, drawn by six white horses, went between the crying, shouting people, down the avenue, and a soft, west wind began to blow like flowers over the faces of the million-faced crowd.

It was a proud day for the people.

That night a lamp burned in the White House in the President's office, and the old General sat with a man who had his back to the light, and threw a long shadow of a beaver hat on the wall.

When Robbie and Davy came in the door, the man rose without turning his face, and went out.

"Who is that?" asked Davy.

"Davy Crockett," said Andy, who would have been powerful lonesome if he had not been full of the strength of the People that day, who tickled his sap and made it rise. "Why, Davy Crockett, you old half horse and half alligator, you ring-tailed roarer, you Chanticleer of the Wilderness. This is your day to crow, Congressman Crockett."

"Old Hickory Jackson, President of the U.S., you tough blossom of the forest, you. I've grinned the bark right off the trees and the hyenas out of the woods, brought the larks out of the sky, and set the pesky Peddlers high tailin' it back East."

"Set, friend," said Andy.

"I guess yore friend who snuck out," said Davy, "was Slickerty Sam, Slackerty Simms, Eight percent Dibble Bartholomew Grizzle Thimblerig Peddler, and I guess with us ganged up and the people pat behind us, he's shakin' worse than the Shake country in an earthquake."

"We'll beat the bush for the game, Davy Crockett, like we used to do. They say we'll run the country into a gopher hole. Ruined past redemption. But we'll make homespun a noble fabric."

"Remember when we had a shooting match," said Davy, "and you shot the hind end off a bee at a hundred yards?"

"It was slightly deflected by one hair of the bee," said

Andy, modestly. "And you shot the whiskers off a wasp at two hundred."

"Oh," said Davy, "I think the shot deflected by a mosquito leg."

And they remembered, while Robbie listened, his head turning to one and the other, till he felt like a myth himself.

Andy said, "Now I've lost my Rachel, my only blood relations are the People."

And his old top-knot seemed to grow red again, and the roar of the people, celebrating, could be heard from the streets, the ballrooms, the taverns, the homes of Washington.

The Trip

THE PEOPLE in the Blue Ridges, the Smokies, the cane-brakes, the workers in the mill, the hod carriers, the shovelers, diggers, making canals that were carrying people west, the farmers, the mechanics, all heard Davy Crockett that year talking in Congress about land for the Indians and land for the poor farmer and squatter.

Jackson was shaking the bank hornet's nest, and Crockett was booming out in Congress, and people filled the balconies and cried, "Hurrah for Crockett!" and the people laughed when they heard the tales about the long speeches by congressmen! "It's nothing to Crockett," they said, listening with pride from the galleries.

"Some men seemed to take pride in saying a lot about nothing. Their tongues go like windmills whether they have grist to grind or not. Others just listen, doing nothing at all for their pay but just listen, day in and day out. But I wish I may be shot if I don't think they earn every penny, considering most of the speeches. That is, provided they don't go to sleep. No one can imagine how dreadful hard work it is to keep awake. Splitting gum logs in August is nothing beside it."

His enemies said he never learned the rules of debate and was awkward, but his speeches are recorded in the *Congressional Record* for you to read. He was easy but far-sighted, and the galleries cheered him. But Davy Crockett drove straight to the point and showed up the dull, windy speeches. He could seize an argument like a panther tail and tie his enemies up in it, and he could make the galleries roar with some backwoods humor. His argument was always warm and alive in behalf of his people, and his poor neighbors of grit and whole hearts.

A great issue had taken new shape—the free lands. The land Davy's grandfather fought for in the revolution had been seized by big land owners who lied about and juggled land titles, and men who had bent their backs to clear the land were robbed of it by Philadelphia lawyers and forced to pay big prices for the poorest land. The grants that were made to soldiers who fought in the Revolutionary War were taken by speculators who claimed the tracts. Settlers who believed they owned the land were, as Davy said, "ransacked, picked and culled till everything valuable had been collected, and they were then moved to patches and scraps of land."

Davy roared on the floor of Congress, "I have seen the last blanket of an honest, industrious, poor family sold under the hammer to pay for unjust and heavy taxes and for the survey of the land itself, and most of the land so poor it wouldn't even raise a fight."

"Amen—That's the ticket," the squatters said, from the galleries and from the clay gullies of his native Tennessee.

He spoke in behalf of his poor neighbors, and Polly and his children in the canebrake. "These men of the western waters," he said, standing tall and talking tall, "these men who have broken the cane. Their little all is to be wrested from them for the purpose of speculation. The titles to the land of these poor settlers are to be sold to the mighty and powerful who never turned a furrow, or built a rail fence, or hunted bear for the hunger of their childers. I propose a low price for that land and a long time to pay, and the squatters' titles recognized. It shall never be said that I sat by in silence."

The people heard his voice, preachers and peddlers took it afoot and ahorseback. Robbie wrote his mother a letter she never got, and couldn't have read if she had. Robbie was going to a reading school in time out from listening to Davy on the floor. People listened solemnly in church, and hall, and tavern, on hunts and frolics, to the words repeated by their own speaker, tongue of them and voice for their silence. "He said that right up to the big fellows," they said. "He's a caution to wildcats. . . . I'll be a ring-tailed roarer myself . . ."

One night as he was walking down the avenue, marveling at how many people could gather in one spot, a gentleman tipped his hat, and said, "May I, sir, accompany you on your walk?"

"You can swing along, partner, on the trail for all of me and welcome."

The gentleman had to run and puff to keep up with Davy. "I heard your speech," he panted. "You're a man of talent. Let us stop at this tavern, I have something to offer you."

Davy stopped and looked down the belly of the velveted and laced cockaded gentleman, the money jingling even when he didn't move.

Across a hot grog he said, "Now, Mr. Crockett, you are not going to let the country go to waste."

"I am not," said Davy. "I aim that the poor and the hoers and hunters shall get it."

"But they don't know how to take care of the country, Mr. Crockett. They are ignorant."

"Ignorant enough to clear the land, water it with their sweat, make the clothes on your back and the very lace around your croaking throat, sir."

"You could bring your wife and children East. I have just the house for you. Now the Red Indians have far too much country."

"It was their country."

"Now, sir, you are too intelligent a man. I can show

you how to buy cheap and sell dear. If we can get that land, beg, borrow or steal it, we can rent it out for cash money."

"Over my dead body, you'll do it," Davy said.

"I know all the ways to make money and I'm finding out some new ways. How much would you take not to vote on your own Squatter and Indian Bill. We got the land, the titles, the Indians, the squatters, the slaves. Come on our side and you can bring your wife east and dress her in velvet. You can live the life of Riley."

"But you ain't got me," Davy shouted. "I'll get a streak of lightnin' and thrash you with it. I'm the yaller blossom o' the forest. You make my liberty sap rise."

Just then the cambric ruffle of the gentleman slipped, and his fat, loose skin shook and dropped. The snake flesh over the eye fell away, and Davy saw the cock-eyes of the Peddler looking at him, and he jumped up, yelling, "Slickerty Sam Thimblerig Bartholomew Grizzle, that tetociously scoundratious, pesky varmint! Stand back, gentlemen, and form a ring. I'm Davy Crockett and I got revolutionary sap, and it's risen in me mighty high. It's thundering along and its gonna break—and I aim to do it. I mean to lay you low."

They tried to hold him, but he was a tornado for sure. He jumped off the ground his whole length, they said, and hit the gentleman like a drop of rain, seized his waistbands and generally discombobolated him, and when they pulled Davy away, the gentleman's lace and cambric ruffles were off, and even his pants were off, and he stood up and said grandiously, "I challenge you to a duel." The tavern howled like a bunch of hyenas.

"Send your seconds," Davy said. "We'll fight with bows and arrows."

On a gale of laughter, the gentleman got a cab, and Davy was swung to the shoulders and proposed for President.

But a sad thing happened when Davy Crockett stood up to fight against the Indian Bill. Andy Jackson was standing on the other side of the fence. Gold had been discovered on the lands granted to the Indians by treaty, and the white men wanted it, and Andy Jackson did not understand about the Indians—he had fought them too much. So he and Davy had to go against each other.

Jackson tried to get Davy to give up going against the bill, but they were both stubborn, and the enemy poured into the gap that the Indian Bill made between them.

The people all overheard him say, "A treaty is the highest law of the land. You are sending the remnants of a once powerful people into country where they who have hunted cannot hunt. You will fritter away their rights. It's wrong. It is not justice. The President is wrong about the Indians and I know it. When he is right I would go for him more than for any man in the whole creation. I'll wear no man's collar. I would rather be an old coon dog belonging to a poor man in the forest than belong to any party that will not do justice to all. It is a wicked unjust measure and I will go against it. Let the cost to myself be what it might. If I should be the only member of the House who voted against the bill, and the only man in the U.S. who disapproved of it, I would still vote against it, and it would be a matter of rejoicing till the day I died. I have a good, honest vote, gentlemen, against the Indian Bill. I will not make me ashamed in the day of judgment."

But he was not the only man against the Indian Bill. There were many against it of every station and place and position.

"It's nothing to Crockett," became a slogan.

He was the People's hero. They always know the face and tongue of an honest man, and honor one who stands alone against power. There was a march of music, the *Crockett March* made for him, played on the streets and blown mightily through the horns of the land.

A grand play was written about him called the *Lion of the West* with a Kentuckian as the hero, named Colonel Nimrod Wildfire and he looked exactly like Davy Crockett, a tall, heroic piece of an actor named Mr. Hackett. Davy and Robbie were invited to come to a gala performance at the theater in Washington where all the ladies would be in their perfume and crinoline, and all the gentlemen of the cabinet (Davy now called it the Kitchen Cabinet!). Davy and Robbie slicked down their natural hair with bear grease, put on a white collar, pared their thumb nails and sat in the box with the People, crying, "Huzza for Crockett!" and they had to stand and bow and grin the knotholes out of the stage wood. Then Mr. Hackett came before the curtain, the spit and image of Davy when he wore his buckskin, and Mr. Crockett bowed solemn to Mr. Hackett, and Mr. Hackett bowed solemn back to Mr. Crockett, and the crowd went wild. It was a hilarious gala evening.

Then something happened that Robbie and Davy wouldn't understand for a little time. Some Very Respectable Gentlemen, and that ought to have roused their suspicions, invited them to go on a tour and meet the people who were clamoring all over the east to see Davy Crockett.

So a grand tour was made for him wherein he should go to Boston and Philadelphia, to Massachusetts to see the new weaving machines that used the slave cotton of the south, to deaf and dumb schools, to insane asylums, to theaters. They even offered him a degree at Harvard University which he declined because he never could wear cap and bells nor be called Granny Crockett. He saw miles of factory girls in New England. He was sitting in a hotel in New York when he heard the fire engine and ran to go, but his host said everyone did not fight fires and he forgot that there nobody knows anybody. He said in New York everyone was pitching out furniture day and night, moving away somewhere else, seemed like a frolic changing. "I would rather risk myself in an Indian fight than venture among these New Yorkers at night," he said. "A miserable place a city is for poor people. I wonder they do not clear out to a new country where every skin hangs by its own tail. The city hall here is brownstone in black and white marble in front, like the fine men here, if they get a fine breast to their jackets, can be fustian behind. They think only the poor look at the rear, and anything you do for poor folks is good enough to look at or eat or wear."

He had his portrait painted, and making his toilet by combing his hair and drinking a glass of brandy, he and Robbie ate their way through five states, going on a train that went twenty-five miles an hour. Robbie put his head out to spit to see how fast it was and the spit overtook him so quick it hit him right smack in the face.

He was presented a seal for his watch chain engraved, "Great Match Race Two Horses at Full Speed," and over them the words, "Go Ahead."

They ate at banquets with groaning tables of meat, boar, venison, beef and sea food they never heard of, with the best of wines and champagne foaming up, "as if you were supping fog out of a trumpet," Davy said.

They stopped at Bunker Hill to see that place that marked the "daybreak battle of our rising glory," Davy told Robbie. "I felt like calling to them to tell me how to help protect the liberty they bought for us with their blood. I resolved to go for my country always, everywhere."

He saw improvements, canals, railroads, rivers and creeks you didn't have to swim or wade. Schools for high and low, free from taxation, and he thought the Americans were a whirlwind tipped with thunder.

He was very genteel and quiet when everyone expected to see half horse and half alligator, and a rip-snorting roarer. He was quiet, and fat with their food as a winter bear, until one night there was a banquet in Philadelphia and Mr. Webster was going to be there and all the bigwigs. Maybe he wouldn't have done it if, coming in on the boat into Philly, the Captain hadn't hoisted three flags to show the People he had Crockett aboard, and as they came in sight of the city and advanced toward the wharf Davy said, "I saw the whole face of the earth covered with people, all anxiously looking toward the boat. The captain and myself were standing on the bow deck; he pointed his finger at me and people slung their hats and huzzaed for Colonel Crockett. It struck me with astonishment to hear a strange people huzzaing for me and made me feel sort of queer. It took me so uncommon unexpected; I stepped on to the wharf where the folks came crowding around me saying, 'Give me the hand of an honest man.' Some gentleman pressed me through the crowd, put me in an elegant barouche drawn by four fine horses and I bowed as he told me, and we moved off, the windows full of people looking out, I suppose, to see the wild men. I thought I had rather be in the wilderness with my gun and dogs, than to be attracting all that fuss."

At the hotel the crowd followed and filled the street

pressing to shake hands with an honest man. Upstairs he walked on a platform, took off his hat and bowed around to the People.

They took him to see the cracked Liberty Bell and he made a little speech to the People who spread all around as far as he could see. The sun came out and a gentle west wind blew, as it had the day of Jackson's election, and Davy, with Robbie standing beside him, said, "I reckon old King George thought they were a thundering fine children that was rocked in it and a good many of them; and that no wonder his redcoats were licked, when the children came out with their soldier clothes on and muskets in their hands. God grant that the liberty tree bough on which this cradle rocks may never break."

They took him in a carriage and five men in beaver hats sat around him, and it was then he began to feel uneasy. He said to Robbie, "Do you recognize anybody?"

Robbie said, "Something smells."

They looked at Mr. Webster who was some shakes and could talk a possum down a tree, but he made a fellow uneasy, as Davy wrote in his book later, "He laughs at a fellow, teases and roasts him until he don't know what ails him nor what hurt him but he can't help limpin'. He is above my bend."

Well, the handsome carriage drove prancing through the streets and all the people followed. The police tried to shoo them away but they followed, and they stood right outside the hotel where the banquet was. Davy and Robbie managed to wave to them from a balcony, but the gentlemen in long coats passed them back as if they were buttered.

And Robbie said, "Oh, ho—something looks like something else now. Do you smell anything?"

And Davy said, "A sort o' so and a sort o' not."

They sat down and as the toasts began, the mask slipped, and you saw the two eyes of the Peddler, who would walk ten miles a day or night for a swindle.

Robbie said, "It's him . . . shall we make it for the window?"

Davy said, "No, we'll blast him with his own thunder." They presented him with a great gun, a long, new rifle.

Mr. Webster made a thundering powerful speech and made little jokes about the strong man of the forest and the canebrake, and Davy saw they had been making sport of him and his people, and he had swallowed the bait hook, line, and sinker. His sap rose to a terrible pitch and he smoked like a tar barrel, and Mr. Webster said he had seen the better of his ways with that yaller flower of the forest, Andrew Jackson—and he delicately wiped his nose of the bad odor and the lace hung from his white hand.

Davy threw the smoking champagne glass across the table and rose and did not drink the toast. Then he offered his own, "Gentlemen, I call you that . . . I know you like a squirrel knows a hickory nut from an acorn, and to know you is harder than climbin' a peeled saplin' heels upward, but I know you now, and I make a toast to you Whigs and Tories. You have been fought by my own grandfather and my son after me will fight you. Here's a toast for you! May the bones of tyrants and kings serve in hell to roast the souls of Tories and Whigs, if it turns out they have souls! Here's to the road leading west —Wilderness Road—and the great journey of the People fighting kings and Peddlers till creation freezes over. And look out for us when we return for we're ring-tailed roarers and a caution to crooks!"

And he and Robbie walked out and down into the street with their people.

And the next day they started back to Wilderness Road where Sally Ann Whirlwind, and a new baby Crockett had never seen, were waiting for them.

Fare Thee Well Awhile

"I SET OUT for my own home; yes, my own home, my own soil, my own humble dwelling, my own family, my own hearts, my ocean of love and affection which time cannot dry up. Here like the wearied bird, let me settle down for awhile and shut out the world."

He and Robbie went to say good-bye to Andy Jackson and Davy told him, "I make a caution to the People not to repose too much power in the hands of a single man. Poor old Andy, you're surrounded by a set of horse leeches, who will stick to you while there is a drop of blood to be got, and their maws are so capacious that they will never get full enough to drop off. They use you to promote their private interest, and for all your sharp sight, you remain as blind as a dead lion to the jackals who are tearing you to pieces. If I am never elected again I will have the gratification to know that I have done my duty.

"They tried to make a clown of me and sell me on the block.

"I went down to Jericho and fell among thieves.

"I guess I was swallowed by my own myth . . . or swallowed my own myth."

Andy said, "Well, you're not elected. Just heard the return; they've beat you. They'll never forgive you, Davy Crockett, and I'm glad you stood against them. I heard it cost them twenty-five dollars a vote to lick you, Davy. They voted everyone twice. They got money to burn."

"Well I beat the Tories up and over Salt river. I followed you, Andy, till you plowed too crooked. My pa told me to plow a straight line to the red cow in the pasture but the cow began to go crooked and so the plough began to plough crooked and my pa balled me out, and I said I was ploughing straight but the durn red cow was a movin'.

"Run down the Mississippi till you come to the Obion river, run a small streak up that, jump ashore anywhere and inquire for me.

"Come to my house. I'll give you a good racoon pie, and bush eels fried in butter, which are dishes my wife cooks. You shall have the softest white oak log to sit on, and the best bearskin to sleep on. I will take you on a coon hunt, and show you how to tree a catamount, and take a blizzard at a bear. You can take a walk in my crab apple orchard and see the alligator pear trees. I will convince you that I can run faster, jump higher, squat lower, dive deeper, stay longer under, and come out drier than any man in the whole country."

"Fare thee well, Davy Crockett," said Andy.

"Fare thee well awhile, Old Hickory," said Davy Crockett.

And Davy Crockett and Andy Jackson never saw each other again.

So he and Robbie started back by river and by stage, and all the animals were lined up on the Blue Ridge waiting for him and all the stage drivers shook his hand and said, "You did your best, Davy, you showed no man had a collar round your neck."

I'm a goin' back to roamin'
Fare you well, traveler, fare you well,
Awhile,
You have traveled many a lonely mile,
You have left behind your bride,
And have no one by your side
So, fare you well, fare you well, awhile.

But my grandmother said that every squatter and Indian in the shakes went out the Wilderness Road to meet him and Robbie.

Going west they could see the land was getting filled up, and Davy told them that the whole country was getting filled up and that anything could happen and practically everything did happen. Men all over were rising like yeast in bread. There were trains—many carriages fastened together with no horses but hot steam pulling them up the highest hills; there was a brisk two way traffic on all the rivers; pick axes, shovels and Irishmen behind wheelbarrows were digging big canals; Mike Fink was seen sitting on the banks of the big shore, weeping, saying, what's the use of improvement. Where's the fun, the frolickin' and the fightin'—gone, all gone.

Settlers were moving west in big pack trains. All the rangers, and general hornswogglers were moving west. Over in Texas they were riding like Mexicans, trilling like Indians, shooting like Tennesseeans, and fighting like the devil.

And they came to the Tennessee Gap and there, through the fall haze, they saw the green valley lying before them, and they left the stage, and Robbie and Davy Crockett walked back into the wilderness.

Without being noticed, they walked into their own clearing. John was chopping wood, and the smoke came out of the cabin chimney, and the children were playing hopscotch on the bare ground. The hounds had got so lazy and fat, they rose slowly as they saw strangers enter the clearing and then they went wild. Polly ran out and they nearly cracked each other's ribs; and the brand-new baby was bawling like sixty. It was a regular hurricane blew up.

The table was agroaning that night with the venison and bear meat John had shot for the winter. He was a hunter now, but never such a hunter as Davy.

That night the neighbors, who had come more close while Davy was gone, came in to hear his tales, and shaking his hand, said, "I voted for you, Davy Crockett. You're our man but they brought voters in, and they took away votes, and they didn't even count 'em. You only lost by a few, but you lost. We're mighty tall proud o' our Davy Crockett," they said, and the fiddlers fiddled, and Davy sat by the fire, telling the tales of the far things he had seen.

"My life has been one of danger, toil, and privations. I have a new row to hoe, a long and rough one, but come what will, I'll go ahead.

"When my grandpappies were hidden in the little ships that took out from Ireland to the shores of America, they fled to the green of Tennessee and Kaintuck, to the big, brawling, go-ahead, splendiferous country, still looking and fighting for freedom.

"I am for those that have never been mastered. I never give up liberty. They can all go to hell and I'll go to Texas."

"No!" said Polly. "Davy Crockett you ain't aimin' to move again!"

"Why, look yourself," said Davy. "This cabin's too small."

It never occurred to Davy, my grandmother said, to build a bigger house, only find a bigger country.

"Why we got to get there first."

"But Texas belongs to the Mexicans," Robbie said.

"Why, it belongs to who settles it. Times are getting poor. I saw the killdeers flying over that poor land worn out already. The game gone, you couldn't raise a fight on the land. The apples are so ornery small, the pig when he puts his tooth in one lays back and hollers. The hounds are so lean and lopsided they have to prop them up against a tree before they let 'em bark."

Polly wept for the first time in her life before anybody, and they all sat solemncolly.

"Never mind," said Davy, "I'm not going tomorrow. We're going on a slam-bang, up-and-coming, derring-do Elk hunt before I'm gone. We'll come out hollering in the sun. I'm the Chanticleer of the Settlement.

"Don't lag behind," he told his neighbors of grit and whole hearts. "We're heading toward the millennium. Who wants to be left out? The weight's liften' from man and he will rise. It's a new world, not stopping. Everything will and must get better."

And all the Crocketts answered, "Then go ahead."

So the next morning early the hounds were baying and edgy to be off. "The dogs know there's no mistake in me," said Davy to Polly, as he gave her a hug, and hugged all the chilluns, and set off for the last time with his sons, John and Robbie, walking on each side of him, and the hounds with their red tongues lolling, yipping ahead.

He found Betsy, where he had greased her, laid her

away. He didn't carry his new gun but took the old piece. "I love her," he said, "for she and I have seen hard times together. If I hold her right she always sends the ball where I tell her. She mighty seldom tells me a lie. My dogs and I have had many a high time of it with old Betsy."

John and Robbie and Davy walked along the deep cane, and the sun fell down, as Davy said, "like gold from the Biddle's treasury." And Davy wanted to talk to his tall sons who walked silent and sad with him.

"My thermometer," he said, "is below freezing point to leave you."

"It makes a thawing in the eyelids," Robbie said.

"Is it the right grit to leave your poor country?" Davy asked.

"Well, you have to know what is right."

"Then go ahead," they said, but there was no grin in them.

"Blast my corn shucking soul," Davy said, and they passed right by a fat bear looking at them. "I first ran away east as a vagabond boy. I walked there on my moccasins, and I drove there in the new steam buggy. I been bound out like a slave, and I been to Congress. I brushed beaver in Virginia and didn't get paid a coonskin; I been foxed, fleeced, skinned and starved in the wilderness. I been to the bottom of the river and I can stay down longest.

"I been in the lonely lonely, with the waggoners singing

and laughing and calling down the mountain, traveling the dark familiar gap into the wilderness that leads—where?"

All his life a dancer, Davy Crockett now tried to say something to his sons, before going to his death at the Alamo. He was still bold, tall, and free and now bent only like a good stout tree in a strong wind, and his two sons, green saplings feeling no wind yet, listened as they sat on a log and the hounds bayed in the distance.

"I've been to the great frolics of the People, after the grain and the flax were reaped. Nobody could dance longer, sing longer, or get into more scraps than yore pappy, Davy Crockett.

"But now I got to go down to Texas, for there are foxes in the grapes, and hyenas in the corn.

"Like everybody, I've been a Nero and a clown, a wag and a tragedian, and when I was sitting in that box with the people smiling and waving and stamping their feet, yelling, 'Huzza for Davy Crockett!' I saw myself on the stage and Mr. Hackett, the spit and image in buckskin and fringe and coonskin cap and all. I stood and bowed to myself, with myself bowing back, and it was to laugh.

"I've seen men making a mighty dollar, with codfish timber and rum; I've seen hunting parsons and scarlet-robed judges, and fat men in six-horse gilt carriages. I've seen land offices and law courts run elections. I've seen Negro and indentured white slaves, without learning, some without vote. You can see a mighty lot just walkin' the Wilderness Road, in moccasin or buckskin.

"I've wasted some myself, killin' more animals than I could eat. Left their carcasses to the buzzards, helped poor the land and the forest too.

"I don't know the right of it.

"The great tree of America has many roots, some solid and some bad. Knee breeches, silk stockings, silver buckles control you lock stock and barrel so you keep going west. Now they're booting us into the country of the Mexicans, and it's dog eat dog any way you put it.

"You got freedom, but its freedom for to grab the land. Gab and grab, that's the ticket. Nobody knows how to put the bit and rein. Go ahead, I say, but there are those I see now who go ahead and take the bark off the trees, take the trees, take every man jack of us like a slave. I don't know the right of it."

My grandmother said Robbie couldn't remember it all but when Davy's diary was found in Texas, he had written this in it:

"Universal independence is an almighty idea, far too extensive for some brains to comprehend. It is a beautiful seed that germinates rapidly and brings forth a large and vigorous tree, but like the deadly upas, we sometimes find the smaller plants wither and die in its shades. Its blooming branches spread far and wide, offering a perch of safety to all alike, but even among its protecting branches we find the eagle, the kite, and the owl preying upon the helpless dove and sparrow. Beneath its shades myriads congregate in goodly fellowship; but the lamb and the fawn find but frail security from the lion and the jackal, though the tree of independence waves over them. Some imagine independence to be a natural charter to exercise without restraint, and to their fullest extent, all the energies, both physical and mental, with which they have been endowed; and for their individual aggrandizement alone, without regard to the rights of others, provided they extend to all the same privilege and freedom of action. Such independence is the worst of tyranny."

Robbie said it looked to him like to go to Texas was to invade the country of the Mexicans. And Davy said they had invaded and he was fighting the tyrant. It was a caution to wildcats.

Davy was silent and didn't even follow the baying of the dogs that had treed something. He said, "Sorrow, I guess, could make an oyster poetical. I knew I wouldn't be able to talk nothing straight so I wrote a poem."

But just then the eight dogs were singing out clear as a bell.

The three ran and then they stopped, five deer were coming toward them as if they had never seen a human being before, but the two elk had fled with the dogs after them. They walked for more than an hour after watching the high trees, where the elk had nibbled, listening to the dogs.

"There," said Robbie. And there they were, the two great beasts feeding in an open space, restless and shy. The sun was down and it was dim and dodging among the trees, they got one of the elk within range, the other

running among the dusky trees, stopped, wheeled. Robbie fired and missed. The elk moving toward him, suddenly pawing the ground and shaking his head, with his great horns branching six feet high and wide across, lowered angrily, pawing and then suddenly crashing forward straight at Robbie. Robbie raised his hands, gave a shrill high cry, and the elk wheeled and like darkness itself, disappeared.

"Wait and let the dogs open." Everything was quiet. Robbie knew this would be the last hunt with his father, and he saw him like the old Crockett, his powerful and tremendous self standing at bay in the darkening forest most beautiful, powerful and swift, poised behind the gun sight of his old gun, Betsy, and he knew no one, not even Sam Slick could take away his deed and title to himself.

Nearly an hour passed, then Whirlwind opened, howled twice, and Rattler gave a long howl. Then the others joined. Davy cried, "He's up, he's up," seized his rifle, and they all ran toward the roar of the dogs. John's gun went off, which caused the dogs to swerve but not for long. They came on driving the great Elk back to the guns.

They ran a quarter of a mile toward them, then heard the dogs making the bend as though they were turning and the bushes ahead broke lower down. Then, not one but two Elks burst out of the cane, a buck and a doe a hundred and fifty yards below him.

"I have him," Davy said, and waited now for that moment. They came down the open glade of the twilight, then there was a moment when even the dogs were still. Davy leveled the gun, fired and the big buck turned, startled, buckled at the knees and the great antlers went down to the ground like a great fallen tree.

Davy, John and Robbie ran to the great buck, hearing the doe crying and running through the cane.

The dogs were beside themselves with excitement. "I don't think I ever heard the hounds give such music. Old hunter as I am, it makes my hair stand right on end." The dogs wouldn't let the great creature be touched. They lay against the buck for a time and would not let even Crockett touch him. Later when the dogs were sleeping, full of blood and meat, the three men roasted fresh meat around the fire. The hunt had been beautiful.

Robbie said, "You said about the poem—"

"Well," Davy said, shamefacedly, "it's zigzag as a worm fence. I guess Davy Crockett can write a poem, got a right to write as well as Mr. Longfellow. I'm a long fellow too."

"Go ahead," they said.

Farewell to the mountains whose mazes to me
Were more beautiful far then Eden could be;
No fruit was forbidden, but Nature had spread
Her bountiful board, and her children were fed.
The hills were our garners . . . our herds wildly grew,
And Nature was shepherd and husbandman too.

I felt like a monarch, yet thought like a man,
As I thanked the Great Giver, and worshipped His plan.

The home I forsake where my offspring arose;
The graves I forsake where my children repose.
The home I redeemed from the savage and wild;
The home I have loved as a father his child;
The corn that I planted, the fields that I cleared,
The flocks that I raised, and the cabin I reared;
The wife of my bosom—farewell to ye all!
In the land of the stranger I rise or I fall.

Farewell to my country! I fought for thee well,
But I am cast off . . . my career now is run
And I wander abroad like a prodigal son—
Where the wild savage roves, and the broad prairies spread,
The fallen—despised—will again go ahead!

No one spoke. Even the beasts were silent. Robbie heard an acorn fall alone and silent in the forest—a little sound.

"Well," Davy said, rubbing the ears of old Whirlwind. "I'm going to cut and quit. I leave the myth to you. We are all myths. I am now on my journey to leave my home, my neighbors, friends, and country for a strange land. I don't know the right of it, blast my corn shucking soul. I'll go down to Little Rock now, and across into the brazen country and may never return. Anything that would render death to a brave man particularly pleasant, it is freedom. I'll dress in my new, clean hunting shirt your ma is amaking, put on my new foxskin cap with the tail hanging down, Robbie here made me, and my new Betsy rifle, I'll start down the Big Muddy and go ahead in the world."

And his sons said, "Go ahead."

And the hounds all said, "Go ahead."

And he went ahead, but now he was not sure.

Remember the Alamo

Being the last days of Davy Crockett; he goes down the river with four strange friends—Thimblerig, the Bee Hunter, the Pirate, the Indian. Concerning a mustang that ran away; a buffalo hunt; a fight with outlaws. The fight against Santa Anna at the Alamo. The Funeral Pyre. Sunrise in his Pocket.

Journey Into the West

SO POLLY Ann Whirlwind and all the big and little Crocketts waved good-bye to Davy Crockett in the fall; and he took a little boat down the Obion to the Mississippi, to go to Arkansas, and on to the Brazos and on over the green plains of the new Republic of Texas, to fight another tyrant at the battle of the Alamo.

As usual, he made up a tall tale, as he saw his big sons, John and Robbie, who would go to school in Jackson that winter and learn things Davy had never known; he had to tell them—"I'll buckle on my old scythe to carve any tyrant up! I'll sharpen my teeth on a flying millstone, bolt up a little Yankee lightnin', and bridle the old bear, and strike out like a hurricane for Texas. My old bear full of indignation will sweat and make the rocks and trees fly behind him, and the very hair o' creation will stand straight up in double distilled wonder. By the time we land in Texas, his eternal speed will scald all the prairie and set my buckskin to steamin', and the very ground and trees will know us and shout, 'Eternal Freedom, for Davy Crockett's come!' "

But the truth of the matter was that he felt very low after he saw his family for the last time and he didn't know if he was right or not, but he was going ahead! And the truth was that he had a maddening slow journey in a fancy Mississippi boat that floundered down that wicked, crooked river, which begun to curve, flow backward, and change its bed in the night. But at last they came to Little Neck in Arkansas and the people, hearing of Davy Crockett's arrival, met him with fife and drum and came out to see Crockett, "the real critter," and fed him up proper and gave him a little mustang to carry him to the Alamo.

In the evening he wrote to Robbie, who could read now, saying, "We went through a tall forest. I had left my country now and felt somewhat like an outsider, neglected and lost sight of. We were alone in the wilderness, and the old man riding with me checked his horse and a stream of eloquence burst from his aged lips, such as I have seldom listened to. We were alone in the wilderness. It seemed as if the tall trees bent their tops to listen; that the mountain stream laughed out joyfully as it bounded on like some living thing; that the fading flowers of autumn smiled, and sent forth fresher fragrance as if they knew they would come out in spring, and even the sterile rocks seemed to have some mysterious influence. My strength and courage were renewed."

Later in the diary that was found near his body at the Alamo, he told about his trip; how he met up with a peculiarsome fellow, named Thimblerig, who sat all day with three thimbles and a pea, looking mighty like the Peddler, but who came along to the Alamo giving up his bad ways, and fighting with Davy for freedom; and a singing Bee Hunter, a merry fellow, joined them along with a Pirate, with a scar along his cheek, who had fought with Old Hickory at New Orleans, and an Indian who was going to fight Santa Anna, who had taken his land.

Davy tells about the adventure when the little mustang met a group of his wild friends and took off with Davy on his back, over the prairie, and how he met up with some of his old Indian friends, the Comanches, and went on a great buffalo hunt with them.

Crockett is said to have visited several Indian tribes, many Choctaws, Creeks and Cherokees, who had been dislodged from their homes and had, like Crockett, come to find new ones, and remembered him as the man who had both fought them and fought for them.

One day they heard a queer fiddling coming from afar, and as they approached on their horses, the tune changed as if someone was fiddling every tune he knew. Reaching the river crossing, they saw an old man, with a long white beard, seated in a sulky in the middle of the river, playing a fiddle for all he was worth—the high river pouring around him clear over the haunches of this thin old horse.

"You've missed the ford," they yelled at him.

"I know it," he said.

"If you go ten feet further you'll be drowned."

"I know it, I can't turn back."

"Then how'll you get out?"

"Don't know, that's why I'm fiddling to the fishes. In times of peril I always fiddle, because, as a parson, I know there is nothing in universal nature so well calculated to draw a crowd together as the sound of a fiddler's tune. I might shout myself hoarse and nobody would stir a peg."

Davy rode out, turned the sulky around, brought the old man to shore.

"Thank ye," he said, "I'll preach a sermon if you like."

"Oh no," they laughed. "Oh no, you don't."

Crockett was bidding his friends good-bye at the ford so he went on, with the old man riding beside him as he sat in the sulky, and played all the tunes he knew all over again.

They rode on toward Bexar, San Antonio to the Alamo. They rode through the wide, soft, red land, through the forests with bright green carpets of luxuriant grass, going down to old Camino Real, or Kings Highway of Spanish days, which now was only a mule track. They were called "Crockett's Company," and were a jovial party with gay times wherever they went, dances and story-telling at night—stories of the wonders of Texas. They rode through an expanse of canebrake thirty feet high on a narrow trail where the light slanted in a pale greenish twilight. After many jogging hours, they came out on the broad, brilliant prairie. Three black wolves were running far ahead, too far to shoot. Flocks of wild turkey fanned out on the fanwise plain.

As they came to Nacogdoches, which means pawpaw-eaters, they saw gay white houses lying in a dell, a flag flying from the top of a high liberty pole, drums beating, fifes playing, celebrating a banquet held in honor of two Mexican officers of the Texas Republic for which they were fighting. They had been imprisoned by Santa Anna, and had escaped and were being received with great warmth by the new Republic of Texas, in a town called Washington-on-the-Brazos. They were doing what the Americans had done in 1779, drawing up a Constitution and a Bill of Rights, declaring that all men were created equal and that the Mexicans, the Indians, and the Americans would fight together for a free Republic.

A committee came out on the prairie and asked the five adventurers to join them, and when Davy said that was their purpose, the people went wild, gave him a great banquet, and he took the oath of allegiance to Texas and the Provisional Government. This was January 5, 1836, and Crockett was now a citizen of Texas. After dancing and cutting capers half the night, he sat down and wrote this to his family back on the Obion River:

My Dear Sons and Daughters:

I am in high spirits and have been received with open arms of friendship. Texas is the garden spot of the world, and I do believe it is a fortune to any man to come here. In the pass, where the buffalo pass from north to south and back, is good land—timber, springs, mills streams, range clear water, health, game aplenty, bees and honey aplenty.

I have little doubt to be elected as a member for the Convention to form the Constitution. I am elated. Show this to John and everyone. I hope you will do the best you can and I will do the same. Do not be uneasy about me. I am with my friends.

I must close, with great respect, your affectionate father, farewell,

David Crockett.

The Alamo

IT WAS early in the morning when they came in sight of the fortress of the Alamo far ahead in the green plain, and in the long days waiting the attack, Davy wrote to his family about a skirmish they had with some outlaws and were like to be killed before the big gates of the Alamo opened to let them in.

"We were in the open prairie and beheld a band of about fifteen armed men approaching us at full speed. 'Look out for squalls,' said the old Pirate. 'They are a scouting party of Santa Anna's men.'

" 'And are three times our numbers,' said Thimblerig.

" 'No matter,' replied the old Pirate. 'They are convicts,

jailbirds and cowardly ruffians, who will tremble at a loud word. Let us spread ourselves, dismount and trust to our arms.'

"We dismounted, stood beside our horses to protect us, and waited. They checked their speed, appeared to consult, then spread out their line and came within rifle shot of us. They called out for us to surrender. 'There will be a brush,' said the old Pirate. 'Each of you single out your man for the first fire, and they are greater fools than I take them for if they give us a chance at a second.'

" 'Surrender or we fire," shouted the fellow with the red feather.

" 'Fire and be—,' shouted the old Pirate, at the top of his voice in plain English.

"Sure enough they took his advice and saluted us with a discharge of musketry. Before the smoke had cleared away, we each had selected our man, fired, and I never did see such a scattering among their ranks. They retreated as we hastily mounted and pursued them, which we continued to do until we beheld the Independent flag flying from the battlement of the fortress of the Alamo, our place of destination.

"We rode up to the gates of the fortress, announced to the sentinel who we were, and the gates were thrown open and we entered amid shouts of welcome."

From then on Crockett wrote in his diary:

"I wish I may be shot if I don't go ahead to the last. I write this on the nineteenth of February, 1836, at San Antonio—inside the Alamo.

"We are all in high spirits, though we are short of food for men who have appetites that could digest anything but oppression.

"Colonel Travis, who commands the Texans here in the fortress of the Alamo, greeted us, and knew the Bee Hunter for a valiant man. I found Colonel Bowie of Louisiana here also whose name has been given to a knife of a peculiar construction, made of steel so finely tempered you can split a silver dollar with it. He gave us a friendly welcome and drew his famous knife to cut a string, and I wish I may be shot if the bare sight of it wasn't enough to give a man of a squeamish stomach the colic. He said, 'Colonel, you might tickle a fellow's ribs a long time with this little instrument before you make him laugh.'

"The Bee Hunter was a scout and came back to say he had met some Indians who told him Santa Anna, with a large force, had already crossed the Nueces and might be expected to arrive in San Antonio in a few days. Colonel Travis said he could barely muster one-hundred-and-fifty efficient men, but Santa Anna will have snakes to eat before he gets over the wall, I tell you.

"We set about preparing our defense.

"FEBRUARY 22. The Mexicans, about sixteen hundred strong, with Santa Anna at their head, are within two leagues of the Alamo. We are up and doing and as lively as Dutch cheese in the dog days. The Bee Hunter left this afternoon for scouting.

"FEBRUARY 23. Early this morning the enemy came in sight, marching in regular order, displaying their strength to strike us with terror. They will find they have to do with men who will never lay down their arms as long as they can stand on their legs.

"Our little band entered and secured the fortress and raised our new Texas flag above the battlement, and the Bee Hunter sprightly and cheerfully burst forth, in clear full tone that made the blood tingle, 'Up with the banner of Freedom.' This was followed by three cheers, and drums, and trumpets.

"The enemy took the town, flew a blood-red flag, and sent a message to Colonel Travis asking for his surrender. Travis answered with a cannon shot.

"That night the old Pirate volunteered to try to take a message through the lines to Goliad about four days' march, to let them know we were besieged.

"FEBRUARY 24. The Indian came in the evening, after a battery from the bank was firing at us all day. This afternoon an accident happened to Thimblerig, who was sitting on the parapet practicing his game of thimbles, when a three-ounce ball struck him in the breast. I extracted the ball and told him to wear it for a bauble and he said, 'No, Colonel, lead is getting scarce and I'll lend it out for compound interest, curse the thimbles.'

"At the peep of day, I found Thimblerig alone on the battlement paying his debts, he said, interest and all, closing the account. He had shot four of the enemy. Colonel Bowie was taken sick, and it is only the Bee Hunter who keeps us in spirits with songs and jokes and his daring spirit.

"Last night our hunters brought in some corn. They say the settlers are flying in all quarters in dismay.

"We have given up all hope of help. Colonel Travis told us that if the enemy should carry the fort, to fight to the last gasp. Shell has been falling into the fort like hail. About dusk we saw a man running toward the fort pursued by Mexican cavalry. The Bee Hunter knew him to be the Pirate and, calling to the hunters, we ran out. The Mexicans were close on the heels of the old man who stopped suddenly, shot one of the enemy, ran on, turned, and to the amazement of the enemy, attacked them. Our retreat to the fort was cut off by another detachment of cavalry.

" 'Go ahead,' I shouted, 'Go ahead.'

" 'Go ahead,' shouted the Bee Hunter, and dashed among them. They stood their ground and would have cut us down, but a detachment came from the fort and the Mexicans fled, leaving eight dead. Both the Pirate and the Bee Hunter were mortally wounded, and I received a sabre cut on the forehead.

"The old Pirate died without speaking. We got my young friend to bed, dressed his wounds and he lay until midnight, and he sighed 'Poor Kate of Nacogdoches,' and his eyes filled with tears, and then he sang in a low voice, and I thought of the bright day we rode on our mustangs with the two fresh young voices singing:

But home came the saddle, all bloody to see
And home came the steed but home never came he.

He spoke no more, and a few minutes after, died. Poor Kate, who will tell this to thee!

"MARCH 5. Pop-Pop-Pop, Bom-Bom-Bom through the day. No time for memorandums now. Go ahead. Liberty and Independence forever."

Here ends Colonel Crockett's manuscript.

A friend of my grandmother's, Mrs. Dickinson, was a little girl then, and she and a Negro lad were the only two spared by the Mexicans. She told my grandmother some of what had happened at the end.

There are many stories, and some say Crockett was taken prisoner with five others and brought before Santa Anna who ordered them put to the sword. But Mrs. Dickinson told grandmother this:

"For twelve days the small garrison in the Alamo withstood an army that increased to thirty times its size. The final assault lasted only an hour, and all the defenders were gone, none remained to tell the whole history. Thermopylae had its messenger of defeat. The Alamo had none."

Bowie never got up from his sick bed, and within a few days Travis, too, became ill and Crockett commanded under him. The night of February 24, Travis addressed a heroic document "To the People of Texas and All Americans in the World: I shall never surrender or retreat. Then I call upon you in the name of Liberty to come to our aid. I am determined to sustain myself as long as possible and die like a soldier. VICTORY OR DEATH."

There was no answer. Six days later, when dark had fallen, Travis sent still another messenger bearing a letter to the village of Washington-on-the-Brazos, where Texans including Americans and Mexicans, were writing a Declaration of Independence; and during the night the Mexicans brought up two batteries aimed at the Fort. Travis said that if the enemy took the Alamo they would fight to the last gasp and, as the men cheered, shells fell directly into the Fort. Crockett was everywhere with the swiftness of a hunter, shooting from the parapets, reinforcing the big doors. Amidst the shell they remained all day at their posts without losing a man. At midnight, Travis had his cot carried into the nave of the church and summoned the entire garrison before him. His words rose in the dark naves, and echoed against the mud walls, "We are overwhelmed and our fate is sealed. Within a few days, perhaps within a few hours, we must be in eternity. It is no longer a question of how we may save our lives, but how best to prepare for death and serve our country. If we surrender, we shall be shot. If we try to make our escape, we shall be butchered. To either of these courses I am opposed, and I ask you to withstand the advance of the enemy. When they shall storm the Fort and scale our walls at last, let us slay them as they come. As they leap over the ramparts, slay we all of them until our arms are powerless to lift our swords in defense of ourselves, our comrades, our country. Every man must make his own decision. Do as you think best, each of you. Those who consent to remain with me to the end will give me joy unspeakable."

Helped by Crockett, Travis rose, and with his sword drew a line across the floor.

"Those who will remain and fight until we die, step across this line to my right."

Crockett stepped over.

James Bowie asked his friends to carry his cot across.

Thimblerig tipped his white hat, that now had a bullet hole in it, and stepped beside Crockett. Every man but one stepped across. No one interfered with his departure, and nothing again was ever heard of him.

Five thousand of the enemy now assembled outside the Alamo walls. They had ladders, crowbars, axes and the hooves of their horses muffled. At the first glitter of dawn, the bugles of Santa Anna sounded, and they drove forward toward Crockett and his men standing on the wall, picking off cavalry leaders and infantry men as they came, and in the clouds of smoke the legion advanced, and the front walls were now rammed. Men swarmed up the ladders. The doors of the church fell, and in a blaze of powder the Texans fought, and when their ammunition gave out they fought with stone and clubs and then their bare hands.

Travis lay over his gun. A story is told that Crockett skipped about between bullets and, as he fired his Betsy time and again, he sang out, "Won't you come into my bower?"

Some say he fell on the last parapet with Thimblerig at his feet. However it was, there was a moment when he must have thought of all the green hills of home, all his grown and little children and Polly Ann Whirlwind, and looked beyond the din of smoke to the blue buffalo clover fresh after rain, the red bud, and wild plum feathering in the brush, the acacia golden in bloom.

There came the moment when all that was Davy Crockett, made from the earth, from the flesh of others, his tall, spired brain, his panther heart of imagination, fell down, and all at the Alamo were lost in that final and lonely place. That day a huge pyre was built with cords of wood, and the bodies of the defenders were destroyed and by the charred walls of the Alamo, the tall flames could be seen for miles across the Texas prairie.

"*Remember the Alamo*" became the cry of the Texans as they fought to make a Republic. But Texas was a great prize to others beside Santa Anna, and ten years later the Big Peddlers saw it was a prize of land and destroyed the independent Republic, making a Mexican war to get Texas. And another tall man, Abraham Lincoln, stood up on the floor of Congress and voted against such a war of aggression. Davy Crockett would have sure liked him.

Davy would have been pleased with a song about a gray goose made up about him, which was like one of the wild geese his grandpappy had been, to fight for Ireland's freedom:

Remember gallant Crockett's bones
Have found a glorious bed there.
Then tell them in your thunder tones,
No tyrants feet shall tread there.
Come gather east, come gather west,
Come round with Yankee thunder.

It was sung at many a lively frolic. Like his ancestor, the Huguenot Crocketagne, he had for his crest the wild goose, for its high flight, its grace of motion, its power of wing, and for the fact that it flies against the wind.

From the gayest courts of Europe to Ireland to the struggle against tyranny there, to Virginia and another fight in the American Revolution, and going farther, farther west to fly to one of the great battles of history, flying in one way or another against the wind—the great, gray goose, Davy Crockett.

My grandmother said it was a sad day, many months later, when back on the Obion a hunter told Polly of Davy's death, and handed her his diary of the Alamo, which ended "Go ahead. Liberty and Independence forever."

This same old hunter, in the evenings, before the cabin fire, with hounds sleeping, used to make this sad song for his friend, Davy Crockett: "There is a great rejoicing among the bears of Kaintuck, and the alligators of the Mississippi roll up their shining ribs to the sun, and have grown so fat and lazy that they will hardly move out of the way of a steamboat. The rattlesnakes come up out of their holes and frolic within ten feet of the clearings, and the foxes go to sleep in the goose pens. It is because the rifle of Crockett is silent forever, and the print of his moccasins is found no more in the woods. His old fox-skin cap hangs up in the cabin, and no hunter ever looks at it without turnin' away his head and droppin' a salt tear.

"Luke Wing entered the cabin the other day and took down old Killdevil to look at it. The muzzle was half stopped up with rust, and a great green spider run out of it and made his escape in the cracks of the wall. The varmints of the forest will fear it no more.

"The Colonel had fallen like a lion struck by thunder and lightning. He does not speak again. It is a great loss to the country, and the world, and to ol' Kaintuck in particular. There never was known such a member of Congress as Crockett, and never will be again. The panthers and bears will miss him for he never missed them.

"His screams and yells are heard no more, and the whole country is clouded with a darkness for the gallant Colonel.

"He was an ornament to the forest, and were never

known to refuse a drink to a stranger. When he was alive, it was most beautiful to hear his scream coming through the forest; it would turn and twist itself into some splendiferous knots, and then untie itself and keep on till it got clear into nowhere, and twisted like a big old river to the hearts of the people. But he is a dead man now, and if you want to see old Kaintucks' tears, go there, and speak o' her gallant Colonel, and there's not a human but what will turn away and go behind some tree and dry up their tears. And all the animals will weep, the hounds lag behind, their tails under, old Mississippi Buff and Bear Hug howl in the wilderness and sing mighty hymns, with the great tall trees making a mighty pipe organ, and the hurricanes blowing up a mighty music enough to split the ear drums, playing, farewell—farewell for awhile.

"He is dead now and may he rest forever and a day after."

Sunrise in His Pocket

UP SPRANG one of the loveliest stories of Davy Crockett, told by him most likely, but watered dearly by the springs from the hearts of that Old New Deep Shallow Clear Muddy Straight Crooked river of the People of great grit and whole hearts.

It's the story of the Deep Cold.

"One January morning it was so all-screwin' up cold that the forest trees were so stiff they couldn't shake, and the very daybreak froze fast as it were tryin' to dawn. The tinder box in my cabin would no more ketch fire than a sunk raft at the bottom of the sea. Seein' that daylight were so far behind time, I thought creation was in a fair way for freezin' fast.

" 'So,' think I, 'I must strike a leetle fire from my fingers, light my pipe, travel out a few leagues and see about it.'

"Then I brought my knuckles together like two thunder clouds, but the sparks froze up afore I could begin to collect em—so out I walked and endeavored to keep myself unfriz by going at a hop-step-and-jump gait, and whistlin' the tune of *Fire in the Mountains*! as I went along in double-quick time. Well, after I had walked about twenty-five miles up the peak o' Daybreak Hill, I soon discovered what was the matter. The airth had actually friz fast in her axis, and couldn't turn round; the sun had got jammed between two cakes of ice under the wheels, and there he had bin shinin' and workin to get loose, till he friz fast in his cold sweat.

" 'C-r-e-a-t-i-o-n!' thought I. 'This are the toughest sort o' suspense, and it mustn't be endured—somethin' must be done, or human creation is done for.'

"It was then so antedeluvian and premature cold, that my upper and lower teeth and tongue were all collapsed together as tight as a friz oyster. I took a fresh twenty-pound bear off my back that I'd picked up on the road, and beat the animal agin the ice till the hot ile began to walk out of him at all sides. I then took an' held him over the airth's axis, an' squeezed him till I thaw'd it loose, poured about a ton of it over the sun's face, give the airth's cog-wheel one big kick backward, till I got the sun loose, whistled, *Push Along, Keep Movin'*! an' in about fifteen seconds the airth give a grunt, and begun movin'

—the sun walked up beautiful, salutin' me with sich a wind o' gratitude that it made me sneeze. I lit my pipe by the blaze o' his top knot, shouldered my bear an' walked home, introducin' the people to fresh daylight with a piece o' sunrise in my pocket.

MERIDEL LE SUEUR was born in Murray, Iowa in 1900 and has spent most of her life in the Midwest. Her father was the first Socialist mayor of Minot, N.D.; her mother ran for Senator at age 70. After studying at the Academy of Dramatic Art in New York, the only job she could find was as a stunt artist in Hollywood. Her writing career began in 1928 when the populist and worker groups were re-emerging. While writing stories in the early thirties which gained her a national reputation, she reported on strikes, unemployment frays, breadlines, and the plight of farmers in the Midwest. She was on the staff of the *New Masses* and wrote for *The Daily Worker, The American Mercury, The Partisan Review, The Nation, Scribner's Magazine,* and other journals. Acclaimed as a major writer in the thirties, she was blacklisted during the McCarthy years as a radical from a family of radicals. Among her many published works are *North Star Country, Crusaders, Corn Village, Salute to Spring, Rites of Ancient Ripening, The Girl* and *Ripening: Selected Work, 1927-1980.* The books for children by Le Sueur include *The Mound Builders, Conquistadores, The River Road: A Story of Abraham Lincoln, Chanticleer of Wilderness Road, Sparrow Hawk, Nancy Hanks of Wilderness Road,* and *Little Brother of the Wilderness: The Story of Johnny Appleseed.*

GAYLORD SCHANILEC began his career in illustration by freelancing for several small presses, among them Coffee House Press, Milkweed Editions, and New Rivers Press. Schanilec's most recent finished work is the product of the Jerome/MCBA Book Arts Fellowship Competition, a fine letterpress book entitled *Farmers. Farmers* consists of interviews with Upper Midwest farmers, accentuated with multi-colored wood engravings of their homes. Schanilec is also the creator of the highly acclaimed book *High Bridge*, selected for inclusion in the American Institute of Graphic Arts 1988 Book Show.